Love Me Like That

A Novel Written by Faye

Published by Bright Beginnings Publications

www.brightbeginningspublications.com

ISBN: 978-0-9862294-5-9

Instagram: @fitnessbyfaye

Twitter: novelsbyfaye

Email: novelsbyfaye@gmail.com

storage and retrieval system, without the written permission from the publisher and writer.

Cover Design/Graphics: Michael Horn

Editor: Shalonda Johnson

Proofreader: Ebony Finley

Dedication

This book is dedicated to my younger sister, Adrienne "Sin City" Stevens. This angel was called to heaven too soon, but we all know God doesn't make mistakes. Adrienne has been my motivation to continue to follow my dreams no matter how impossible they may seem to others. Though she is no longer here with me in the flesh, she will live in my heart forever.

I also dedicate this book to my nieces, nephews, and God-daughters. Always follow your dreams, don't allow anyone to diminish your value, and no matter how old you are keep working towards your life's goals. You CAN accomplish greatness; just believe you can like I believe in YOU!

Acknowledgements

To my Lord and Savior Jesus Christ, thank you for the strength to go on when I wanted so many times to give up and quit life. I thank you for sending your angels to protect and guide me through my journeys.

To my supportive parents, Jimmie and Carolyn Stevens. Thank you for always believing in me. The lessons that were instilled in me as a child have helped me to be the woman I am today. I am a woman of wisdom and determination and I thank you and I Love You!

To my sons JaQuan and Tony Jr, thank you for your selflessness. I appreciate your kind hearts and understanding ways. Thank you for sacrificing your time with me and leaning on each other.

To my sisters, Annie and Tajuana, thank you for always believing in my dreams. You never doubted I could get this done and that means a lot to me. You ladies are my rock and know that as I conquer so will you!

To the greatest best friends I could ever ask for, LaSonya and Cassandra. Thank you for always having my back with love and encouraging words. Our un-wavering friendship has stood the test of time. I love both of you and appreciate you more than my words could ever express.

My angel Shalonda. You came into my office and started me on this journey to making my dream of writing a reality, thanks for all of your encouragement through this process. Thanks for pushing me to never give up!

Last but not least, thank you Shawn. You came into my life at a time when I had given up on love and happiness. You brought your laughter and business sense to our friendship and made me see my full value. You believed in me and pushed me beyond my comfort zone in so many areas of my life. I love you and enjoy sharing my life with you.

LOVE

ME

LIKE

THAT

BY:

Faye

Chapter 1

"Tap, tap, tap," I hear a very faint tap at the door that sounds like either the wind blew hard or someone just pushed up against the door. I get up from the couch to look through the glass on the wooden front door and just as I figured, my boyfriend, Derrick of two years was beckoning for me to let him in. He always knocks very softly so that our family's zealous pet dog Wooly doesn't start barking to alert the family of his presence.

"Faith!!" my mother yells from the family room in the back of the house, where she spends a lot of her time once she gets home from her job as a medical assistant at a rehabilitation home. I answer, "Ma'am!!!" screaming at the top of my lungs, but all along not being able to take my eyes off of Derrick. He enters the house in a smooth and slow manner. His cool personality fills the room along with his fragrant cologne. I check Derrick out from head to toe; he has on red Levis; a red t-shirt; red, white, and blue All Star gym shoes; a red, white, and blue starter coat, and a red belt with a big buckle that reads his name, DERRICK. I look up into his eyes and say "hi" with googly eyes and butterflies in my stomach. We live in the same neighborhood in the great city of Chicago and see each other every day, but I am always in awe of his beautiful caramel skin and the deep waves that sit on top of his head… the waves he loves me to rub.

By this time my mom has come into the living room where we are. I could hear my dad stirring in his bedroom next to us. Our house is not that big, but it has just enough room for us; two bedrooms on the first level and two in the finished basement, which is where my siblings and I spend most of our time. It is set up just like a small apartment and makes us feel like we are out on our own. It even has a small kitchenette with a refrigerator and microwave for our snacks. My parents allow Derrick to come and visit in the evenings after my chores and homework are done. It is the exact same time each day, never fails. My dad walks past and says, "How you doing young man?" Derrick nods and says "Hello Sir".

I have four siblings: three sisters and one brother. My dad is a man who takes very good care of his family. Medium height in stature, light-skinned with naturally curly hair, but to me he looks ten feet tall with shoulders big enough to carry the world. He works nights so this appears to be the time where he and my mom change shifts and he leaves us, only to reappear again around three in the morning. My dad pays the bills, buys all the food, and does most of the cooking. In my eyesight, he can do no wrong- and for him, neither can his girls! When I am grown, I want a husband just like my dad: loving, caring, and a provider. My mom is so lucky! He treats each one of us like little angels and always lets us know how special we are to him by playing with us, allowing us to climb in bed with him during rainstorms, and mostly surprising us with treats from his candy warehouse job that he has been at for many years. Even though Derrick is at my house, when my dad is in the room, he is the only one who has my attention. I am seventeen and the fourth child, but around my dad I feel that I am his one and only baby girl.

When my mom sees that I have company and my dad scurries by her because he slept too long, she retreats back to the family room to watch her evening shows. Back there she is away from the commotion of kids and close to the refrigerator where she can refill on her favorite Orange Crush Pop. Most of the time when my dad comes in from work he cooks himself breakfast and even puts dinner in a slow cooker while he takes his first of several naps. By the time we come home from school and my mom gets off of work dinner is ready. Today, we're having beans with smoked hamhocks, fried chicken with brown homemade gravy with onions, white rice, and skillet cornbread. The aroma fills the house each day as we come in from school. It is always a full course meal no matter what day of the week it is. Minutes later my dad reappears to the front of the house with his lunch bag, looking for his keys. "Tiny, have you seen my keys?" I cringe because my family knows how I feel about them calling me by my nickname in front of other people. But since it is my dad, it's okay. I quickly get up to help him look for the keys and we stumble across them on the dining room table under the mail at the same time. "I'm gone," my dad yells loudly. My little sister Alisa, who is seven years younger than me, and my other sister Tonji, who is three years older, appear to say goodbye to him. I walk over to my dad and give him a huge hug as my entire body wraps around him to hold on for dear life. I am very petite at 90 pounds and only 4'11 so my dad slightly bends down and smacks a big kiss on my forehead as he rushes out the door. "Lock the door, little girl," he commands as he exits. I move quickly to do exactly what he said as Wooly almost knocks me over to get to the small side window so he could watch his master get into the car. My brother Jesse lives with us too, but is hardly ever home and my sister Angie, who is the oldest child, left home as soon as she graduated high school to join the Army and travel the world. We don't get to see her very much, which sometimes makes us sad.

As I head to the couch where Derrick is sitting, he says, "Your dad has you rotten." I think about what he says, but really don't care. Derrick calls it spoiled, but my dad just loves us dearly and takes care of his family.

Chapter 2

The summer after my senior year of high school comes to an end. Derrick and I are starting to worry about how we will spend time together once our busy schedules of college and work begin. Derrick is one year older than me and graduated high school the year before me. He loves his job as a UPS courier driver and hopes to start college soon. I will be attending City College in the evenings and working as a gas station attendant during the day. My dream was to go straight into the army after high school. I even took four years of J.R.O.T.C. in high school to train, but decided against it right before graduation. I fell madly in love with Derrick and could not risk losing him by traveling all over the world; I'm sure he felt the same way.

When fall began, the leaves on the trees weren't the only things changing. Derrick and I were barely spending time together and when we did, it was into the early morning hours, which didn't make my parents happy at all. Derrick lived at home with his mom and little sister, so he was the man of the house. His mom did not work so their house was always very neat and dinner was prepared by the time he and his sister came home. His mom was real cool. She was several years older than my parents, but didn't really have an old school mind set. She allowed me to be at their house as much as I wanted to and even gave us privacy in the back of the house where we spent most of the time watching TV... in Derrick's bedroom. Derrick's room was the biggest in their three-bedroom apartment. We would lounge in his double-decker full size bed and watch the twenty-six-inch box TV that sat on his dresser. He also liked to work out a lot so there was a weight bench that sat smack in the middle of his room where I sometimes sat when I didn't prefer to be on his bed.

For the past year, Derrick and I have gotten really close and talked about almost everything. Even when he felt that he was ready for us to take our relationship to the next level, he waited patiently until I was ready. Spending time alone in his room was not always the best situation. Sometimes I could feel the pressure building after a kiss or two along with wandering hands. I was still a virgin, but didn't succumb to his advances… well at least not until the end of my senior year when I felt that I couldn't persuade him to wait any longer. On this day, his mom and little sister were away visiting other family members. I came by his house after work and we both went straight to his room. I was very tired and really only wanted to take a nap before I had to be at home. I guess he wanted to lie down too because he joined me. I snuggled under him and laid my head on his chest. His hands started rubbing my back, then my side, then my butt. He then pulled me even closer and I looked up into his eyes hoping he would see the fear that had come over me; that always came over me when we were in this position. He kissed me gently twice on the lips, then I opened my mouth and our passion exploded. I felt like nothing else mattered but making him happy that I was his girlfriend. He pulled and tugged at my shirt, bra, pants, and underwear as I pulled and tugged for covers to hide my body from him. No one had ever seen me naked besides my family. I always felt that I had a puny body and figured he wouldn't like what he saw. At that point he slowed down and whispered in my ear "do you think you are ready now?" I didn't answer because every time before when he asked, I answered "no". I could feel a sigh of disappointment that covered his body. I didn't want to let him down again so I simply nodded "yes" and closed my eyes. He continued to undress me and climbed on top of me while continuing to kiss me. Then I felt it... his penis touched the most sacred part of my body and I froze. He whispered for me to open my legs and relax but my body wouldn't obey. I was scared; I didn't know what to expect. I would hear girls in high school talk all the time about flips and tricks they did with boys during sex, but I wasn't in an acrobatic mood. After parting my legs slowly, he pushed and pushed until he entered me. It felt like a Q-tip being forced through the eye of a needle. It was not something that I looked forward to doing again at the time, but after a few more experiences and weeks to heal, it was something I started to ask him for.

One late night after spending hours with Derrick he walked me home. We stood on my front porch talking and kissing and talking some more. I heard my mom come to the door a couple of times, but the last time she came she said, "Okay you two, it's two in the morning and both of you have to go to work in the morning." After one more kiss, Derrick headed home and I went inside. When I went in the house, my mom gave me a piercing look out the corner of her eye because it was passed my curfew, but I went straight to my room. When I came home from work the next day, my mom and dad were waiting on me. "Faith, we need to talk to you." I sat down and looked at my dad to try and read how he was truly feeling right now. Of course, as usual, my mom started the conversation with "Well, I will start since your dad is not here most evenings and hasn't really witnessed your behavior." After going on for what seemed like an hour of examples of me coming home late, neglecting chores, and spending too much time with Derrick, the conversation was wrapped up with, "If you can't follow the rules here and you think you are grown, then you need to find another place to live." I searched my dad's face to see if he felt the same way and he just looked away from me and said, "I agree." I tried to apologize for my behavior and for disappointing them, but my dad just insisted that I go to my room to think about my behaviors and determine if I had a decision to make.

Chapter 3

Derrick and I tried to chill out with the late night visits, but it was hard to do since we were only spending a couple of hours a week together now. I missed him so much, all the time. When we were together, we often talked about what our future would be like together, a house, kids, and career goals. One day he asked me about moving in with him and his family; it took me by surprise. I knew that my parents would not agree, but at this point I was eighteen and had done all they ever asked of me, which was graduate high school and not have a baby. Maybe now was time for me to move out…especially since that would allow Derrick and me the opportunity to spend more time together.

Over the following weekend, I got up early, cleaned the house, washed all of my clothes, and studied. When Derrick came over Sunday evening we talked to my mom about me moving out. We explained that I didn't want to keep getting disciplined at home for being out late and how much we just wanted to be together. Since his mom had no problem with it, I didn't think mine would either, but that wasn't the case. She was appalled; her eyebrows raised, her lips tightened, and she stood up. As she towered over us sitting on the couch, almost in each other's laps she addressed me first. "How can you go and live at somebody else mama's house and follow their rules, pay bills, respect them, but can't do it at your own house?" I thought to myself no one said anything about paying bills, but I didn't dare open my mouth. Derrick was the brave soul that said, "My mom has no problem with Faith living with us. She loves her and I will continue to do as I have been doing to help my mom anyway she needs me to." My mom just stared me right in the eyes piercing through all layers of my skin to my innermost soul and said, "Then go." I sat in silence as she turned her back and walked away. I felt so unloved, thinking this is what she has wanted all along... me gone.

Derrick left to go get his friend's car to move my stuff. We had already set a plan of action regardless of if I was staying or moving. Since my mind was made up, I went to pack. My mom went straight into their bedroom and woke up my dad. I tried to listen through the wall as I gathered my things but couldn't hear anything. I slowly emptied every drawer one at a time and gathered all that I owned in the world. By this time, my dad was standing at my bedroom door and I was crying, not really sure if the decision I was making was truly the best. I didn't want to disappoint either one of my parents, but I just felt that it was best for me to move. When I looked up with tears rolling down my face and wiping my nose with a scarf I had just pulled from a drawer my dad said, "Tiny, are you sure this is what you want to do? Because if things don't work out and you ever have to move back home, you will be responsible for paying bills; remember we are not making you leave, this is your..." My heart was so heavy, my stomach was doing cartwheels, my mind contemplating if this would impact the relationship with my dad, but I answered him by saying "yes, I am sure." He said lovingly "Okay, do you need any help?" I kept my eyes focused on the black garbage bag I was putting my clothes into and just shook my head "no" while moving to empty the hangers in my closet.

Chapter 4

Living at Derrick's house was good. His mom didn't bother us and we didn't bother her. We kept right on with our lives as they were, but were now able to spend more time together and didn't really have to answer to anyone. I visited my family as much as time allowed and even picked up my little sister to come hang out where I was living. Our little sisters were around the same age and got along great, so it worked out perfectly. With our daily routines down to a science, time just flew by and before we knew it we were planning a twenty-first birthday celebration for Derrick at his big sister, Beverly's house in the suburbs of Chicago. At the event, family and friends assembled in the basement of his sister's large house. A spread of food on a decorated black and gold table included hot wings, meatballs, spaghetti, tossed salad and a beautiful strawberry-filled butter cream frosted sheet cake. We danced, socialized, and celebrated Derrick with laughter and gifts.

After the family celebration was over, Derrick headed out with his friends and I went home with his mom and sister. Derrick would often go out with his friends and hang out until whenever he wanted to come home. I would sit up waiting for him to come home while allowing my mind to wander about what he could possibly be doing that late when he didn't dance or drink. I started to feel that his friends were more important to him than I could ever be and that us spending time together was no longer a priority because he now had no time for me. Thinking back to the day I left home, my eyes began to water. I could have ruined the relationship I had with my family to spend time with him and now I was neglected and often felt unappreciated. This hanging out was not sitting well with me and I would tell him when he got home. At about 3:00 in the morning our bedroom door creaked open. He stood by the side of the bed undressing slowly and then slid into the bed beside me. I was so happy that he was there that I just swallowed my anger and went to sleep as he nuzzled up close behind me and did the same.

I woke up to him bringing me breakfast in bed and an apology for staying out so late, but I didn't want to argue so I kept quiet. I was still very angry and resented how he took me for granted by not considering my feelings about always going out without me. As the days went by, I struggled to find the words to tell him that I wasn't happy. Five days later, when I finally found the courage to tell him how I felt, he called home to say he was going out with his friends after work again instead of coming home. I was mad, hurt, and confused. Was I not explaining my feelings well enough or did he just not care?

My birthday would be in a couple of weeks. I felt like I needed some space and time away so I called my big sister Angie who was now stationed in Tennessee with her family to see about coming down for a visit. Life for me seemed to change in a way that I could have never imagined. That visit was a pivotal time in my life that seemed to move as fast as the 'L' trains in Chicago. This was supposed to be time away to reflect and think about my life, the way it was, and the way I wanted it to be, but the outcome was far more than I could have ever expected. I had the time of my life with Angie. She was only a few feet taller than me, but her presence filled a room. She commands respect from everyone around and has always been an independent, self-motivated, mature young lady. At ten years older than me, I really look up to her and once upon a time I wanted to be just like her when I grew up. For as long as I can remember, she has had a job and pretty much taken care of herself even while living at home. Her years of traveling in the military seemed to make her even stronger than before, both mentally and physically. She seemed to not depend on or need anyone but herself and made that clear to everyone she came in contact with. During my time with her in Tennessee she showed me the greatest time. We went shopping, had cookouts, and even went to a club for my birthday.

The club was not all that. I thought the lights would be dim, that everyone would be dressed up, and hoped that the men outnumbered the women. The club we went to was small and drab. Nothing like I imagined the clubs of Chicago to be like, but as far as the music was concerned, they played the hits all night long. They even played house music, which was known in Chicago, and many of the guys from my sister's unit took turns dancing with me. I backed my butt up on them and even dropped it down to the floor a few times; they weren't used to my type of dancing so I just kept moving to the fast paced music. This seemed to go on for hours. At one point, when I took a break from the dance floor, I was surrounded by a couple of the men trying to buy me drinks to get to know me better. Finally my sister rescued me. "Come on here birthday girl, let's get you home. You've partied enough for one night," she said. I wasn't ready to go at all, but when big sis spoke, I listened. The next few days I spent a lot of time on the military base at work with Angie. Guys were always everywhere; it was kind of nice to have all that attention since Derrick was always too busy for me at home. I never really had attention from too many other guys. Derrick was my first real boyfriend and I thought he was the be-all and end all. I really enjoyed visiting Tennessee and my sister was fantastic. We spent countless hours during my visit talking about how life was going and our plans for the future. Her listening to me made me feel good. I've always enjoyed our talks and the time we share. My visit was coming to an end, but I was not ready to leave. While I was visiting Angie I didn't have a care in the world. I had only spoken to Derrick a few times, but he called almost every day and Angie would say, "She's asleep," or we just wouldn't answer. I felt that he didn't care about what I was doing when I was back home, so why did he care now. I even extended my visit a few extra days and Derrick was furious when I called to tell him. "Hey, I am having a lot of fun and my sister and I want to do a few more things" I said. "Ok, glad you are enjoying yourself" he said quickly. I then told him, "I'm staying a few more days." The phone went silent and all I could hear was a deep sigh. "What's really going on Faith?" I just want to spend time with my sister and will let you know when I am coming in so if you don't mind can you pick me up from the bus station? "Yep," was all he said then hung up the phone. I later found out that he and his family had planned a surprise party for me, but had to cancel it because I decided to extend my visit.

Chapter 5

I sit looking out the window of this Greyhound bus at families waving goodbye to their loved ones; some smiling and wishing them luck on their new journey and some with tear-stained faces staring into their eyes as if they will never see them again. I know that this will be a long ride back to Tennessee.

After going down there to visit my oldest sister to celebrate my birthday a few weeks ago, I decided to move there. I enjoyed my visit so much that I returned to Chicago, gave my two weeks' notice to my gas station job, and here I am, moving to Tennessee on a trial basis. I am not sure of what the future holds for me on this new journey. All I do know is that my supportive sister and her husband are allowing me to live with them until I get on my feet and find a job. After returning to Chicago with this plan in the back of my head, Derrick and I had a deep discussion about the way things were going for us. As I talked to him with his defensive stance and accusatory tones, I knew it wouldn't end well. It seemed to me like his family and friends were all he needed and he would not miss having me around. Before I left to visit Tennessee we were back to spending as much time apart as we did when I lived with my parents because he hung out a lot with his so-called boys. But of course that story got old because I just couldn't understand why any man would want to hang with other men that much. We went back and forth arguing, me blaming him and him blaming me. We were so loud that finally his mom came in and said, "Now that's enough!" I said, "I agree, I have had enough," and started to pack my things. I packed as much as I could in a plastic bag along with a small suitcase and called my dad to pick me up and take me home. Over the next few days I put my plan into action by first buying my bus ticket back to Tennessee and dropping my classes at the college. Derrick called and came by my job pleading to talk to me, following me to the bus stop in the car, and even embarrassing me by begging me not to leave him openly in front of strangers. One lady even said, "Baby, don't do him like that, look at his face, he looks like he's been crying for days. I'm sure he's a fine young gentleman who may have made some mistakes, give him a chance." Derrick shook his head in agreement with the lady, but we had been through all of this before and I refused to spend the rest of my life being second to anyone or anything. Each time I was around him I avoided eye contact because I did love him but wanted so much more. I enjoyed the attention I got from the guys in Tennessee and knew that when I was ready it would be easy to find someone new. My mind was made up!

The night I was to leave, Derrick and I agreed that I would allow him to take me to the bus station. My dad bought me a huge dark green suitcase and I packed all that I could in it to begin my new journey. I must admit I was afraid of being away from home since I had only ever lived in Chicago, but I knew that my big sis would take good care of me. My bus was leaving at one o'clock in the morning for my twelve-hour bus ride. I talked to my little sister for hours trying to get her to understand why I was leaving and would be back to visit as much as possible and had spoken to my other sister over the phone, but not for long because she was busy tidying up her new apartment and getting ready for her job the next morning. She gave me words of encouragement about doing what I needed to do to take care of myself, but was happy for me and said she wished it were her leaving. My mom and dad walked me to the door of our family's home when it was time for me to leave. I purchased my bus ticket for the weekend to ensure that my dad would be there when I left. Derrick had arrived earlier to take me to the bus station. As I said goodbye to my parents, he took my suitcase and sat in the car. I gave my mom a quick hug and said I would call when I made it, but as I rushed to move to my dad, my mom stopped me, held me away from her by the shoulders sternly, and looked into my face. "Faith, I love you very much. I am proud of the young woman you have become and will always be proud of you. I have only wanted the best for you and you have not disappointed me." By this time I am trying to hold back my tears, but they slowly start to burn my eyes and when I blink they slide down my cheeks. "You kids are the joy of our lives and we never wanted you to leave home, we just wanted you to be focused on your goals" I nodded and said, "I know, ma." She continued by saying how much she loved me and would miss me. I hugged her again and moved to my dad. As he held my hands, he slid money to me and I broke down and cried like a baby. He said, "Tiny, don't leave, just stay here with us. I will help you however you need, you don't have to leave." I said "Daddy I want to leave, it will be okay, I will be okay, you have taught me well and I will continue to make you proud." "I believe that, I love you, Tiny!" he said. "I love you too daddy! I love you both!" I crept down the front stairs of our home contemplating running back in the house and changing my mind, but my feet just kept moving towards the car. As I got in, Derrick passed me a

Kleenex and we drove off with me waving goodbye to my parents.

As soon as we reached the stop sign at the corner of the block, Derrick started in on me. "What, you find some dude down there in Tennessee? Did you sleep with somebody?" All I could do was look at him because he still didn't get it. I was leaving because he was going on with a life that didn't totally include me and I just didn't want that for myself. He went on and on for the full twenty-minute ride to the bus station and by the time we arrived, I knew I was making the right choice. I got out the car, told him I loved him, and grabbed my suitcase from the trunk. I am sure that the suitcase weighed more than me, but I was determined to start my life of independence right now. I said, "Remember that I will always love you" as I walked away dragging the huge suitcase behind me, taking baby steps all the way to the front door of the bus station. When I got to the ramp, a nice older gentleman asked if he could help and pulled the suitcase all the way to the door where my bus would pull in to. When I finally stopped walking, I looked outside and Derrick just stood there with his head down leaning against the car looking lost and disoriented, but I had nothing more to offer him and needed to do what I thought would make me happy.

Chapter 6

After living with my sister, her husband, and two sons in a small three-bedroom house, I was anxious to find my own place in Tennessee. I was working two jobs at the mall, one in a leather store and another at a jewelry kiosk where my time consists mostly of selling costume jewelry and piercing the ears of hollering kids whose parents thought they were simply adorable. I met a friend who seemed really cool while working at the mall. Leslie and I hung out together all the time after work and had a ball. She had a three-year-old son who spent most of the time with his grandmother. Leslie has lived in Tennessee all of her life. Her dad retired from the military and her mom stayed home full-time. Living at home really allows Leslie to party and hang out a lot because there was always someone home to look after her son.

During our many shopping and eating excursions, she talked me in to a double date that I was really nervous about because it had only been about six months since my relationship with Derrick and he was all I really knew for a long time. The way he treated me was all I ever knew about dating and since he was my first for everything, I was nervous about dealing with any other guys.

When we arrived at her house to get dressed, she put on this skin-tight dress that hugged every curve of her not so curvy body and hit mid-way up her thighs. She was much taller than me and thin. She wore hazel eye contacts and a lot of eye makeup. She had her hair in the old salt and pepper style, long on one side and short on the other. She often wears skimpy clothes and flirts with a lot of guys even though she's in a so-called committed relationship. I just put on a light sweater and slacks and she looked at me with a worried frown and said, "Are you wearing that?" Disgust was all over her face and frown lines clearly defined- I was partly offended. I thought my choice of clothing was great. I believe that women should leave something to the imagination and I guess she felt a little differently. We laughed, slipped on our heels and headed to her car. Her description of the evening ahead was that it wasn't officially a date because we were going to hang out at her boyfriend's house to watch some basketball game, but he had a few roommates and I had my choice of them who were all single. At this point, I really felt like we were overdressed. Why was she making a big deal of my clothes if we were only going to watch a ball game? I felt very uncomfortable with this idea because I didn't know what to expect or how this whole get-together had been arranged. "Were they expecting something from me which wasn't about to happen or did these guys even know I was coming with her?" I thought to myself.

When we arrived everyone seemed cool. She plopped into the lap of her boyfriend and I just sat in a big armed chair as close as possible to her acting as though I was interested in the game. There were five guys there including Leslie's boyfriend; they each eye balled us as we walked through the door. The apartment was filled with neutral color decorations; a tan sectional and big chair in the living room with a beautiful maroon and tan oversized rug under the wood coffee table. There was an extra-large mirror against the hallway wall and over the couch was a picture of a half-dressed woman stretched across a beach facing the sunset.

Leslie introduced me to all the guys. One of them, Alton, came over to shake my hand and asked if I wanted something to drink. I said "sure" and followed him into the kitchen. We talked for a few minutes… well I thought we were supposed to be talking but all I did was listen to him talk about his job in the military, how much he likes to work out and how women are all over him every time he goes to the club. He was not all that attractive to me, but it's not always just about the looks for me. He was tall and did have a nice body, was dressed neatly, and was very clean-shaven. But his arrogance was a total turn-off; for Christ sakes, I couldn't have anyone who thought they were prettier than me! I tried to appear to be interested in his conversation, but apparently his other roommate sensed that I needed to be rescued. One of them came over and interrupted our conversation asking if I was enjoying living in a small town like Clarkston coming from Chicago. I asked him how he knew where I was from. He stared into my eyes with a sly smirk on his face, "Just know that I have done my homework." Harold then engaged me in conversation asking me about growing up in Chicago and making the decision to leave. We laughed and talked for a while and apparently after standing back watching us talk with a frustrated look on his face trying a few times to join our conversation, Alton gave up and left. We sat and talked for hours after the game went off while Leslie and her boyfriend retreated to his bedroom. I wasn't uncomfortable with Harold at all. I learned that he was from Texas and had two sisters and a brother but that he was the oldest. He had been in the Army for a couple of years and was enjoying it so far. He ended up having to drive me home because Leslie never resurfaced to even check on me. We made small talk all the way to my house about future goals and aspirations. Then, all of a sudden, I got really nervous because Harold took a lot of back roads and bizarre thoughts invaded my mind of him stopping and raping me then leaving me where I couldn't find my way home. I prayed and before I knew it, we were at my sister's house. He asked me if I would like to go out again and I accepted. He was definitely not the type of guy I would typically be attracted to. He was very light-skinned, only a few feet taller than me, and what I considered to be a little thick. His nice haircut and beautiful smile along with the respectful way he treated me made me feel that he seemed nice enough to give a chance to.

The next day I was floored when at work a big bouquet of red roses arrived through the doors of the leather store being carried by a bouncy blonde girl asking for me. I thought this was some sort of bad joke since I wasn't seeing anyone and assumed Leslie had sent them to say sorry for leaving me alone in a house full of guys to have her one-on-one fun with her man. When I read the card, it said "Thanks for allowing me to spend time with you last night. I hope to see you again soon. - Harold." I had a smile on my face, big as a river and blushing so hard that my manager had to snap me back to reality and remind me that I had customers to tend to. Harold must have remembered throughout our conversation that I said I worked at the mall but I didn't remember giving him my schedule.

As I was leaving work and heading out the mall doors to the bus stop with my roses, I heard someone call my name. I ignored them thinking it was a customer who had read my nametag earlier and I didn't want to be bothered. This gentleman called my name again and said, "Wait girl, it's me Harold." I was happy to see him after the rose surprise earlier, but wondered how he found out what time I got off work. He saw the look of confusion on my face and started to explain that Leslie told him what time I got off work and that I typically took the bus home or my sister would pick me up so he said he took a chance and came up especially because he knew I would have the flowers. He asked if I liked them and my smile from earlier reappeared, displaying all my teeth as I nodded "YES!"

We saw each other for a few months and he always did the nicest things for me; took me out, bought me things, surprised me with small tokens all the time, and cards just to say he enjoyed spending time with me or was thinking about me. As our time together started to turn into a year we were inseparable and seeing him always brought a smile to my face. My sister would even let him spend the night with us sometimes since he lived on the military base and couldn't have overnight guests in his room. I knew that there would only be a little while left for me living there because my sister had just found out she was pregnant and living quarters were already a little tight. She never made me feel that I couldn't stay with them forever, but I was ready to have my own privacy.

Chapter 7

Harold and I sat down with Angie to discuss a plan for us moving in together. We had been dating for a while and were ready to take our relationship to the next step; plus I had just found out I was also pregnant and knew it was time for me to move. Angie was not upset about me being pregnant. As a matter of fact, she was elated at the fact that she would have a niece or nephew to spoil rotten. I was happy too, but very afraid of what it would be like to be responsible for more than myself. Angie discussed with us the importance of a budget, neighborhoods, and laid down rules with Harold for taking care of me like only a big sister could: "Don't mistreat her, don't put your hands on her, and don't play games with her. If there ever comes a time you don't want to be with her just let her know, games are for kids," She said sternly. When we started our hunt for apartments, Angie was right there with me every step of the way. We looked at a couple different places before we decided on a one-bedroom furnished apartment with a walk-in closet and spacious kitchenette. The furnished apartment had a navy blue couch and chair and the dinette set was a cheap-looking table with four small chairs that seemed to be put together with cardboard. Our bed was full-sized with two dressers to match the cream colored headboard. I quickly scoped out the space where the crib would go and allowed my imagination to run wild with a way to decorate the baby's corner of the room with whatever theme we decided on as I got closer to my due date. I was sure it would be either Mickey or Minnie Mouse.

We went on for months so in love, spending time together, watching movies, and mostly preparing for the baby. I loved having dinner ready for him when he came from work most days and taking care of chores that kept our little apartment spic and span. Time was flying by; my two jobs were taking a toll on me because at this point I could hardly see my feet. A big round stomach, round puffy face, and swollen ankles was a far cry from the ninety-eight pound body that I was used to. By this time my sister had delivered my new nephew and I was able to enjoy helping and watching her take care of him. Things weren't the best around her house as far as she and her husband was concerned so I often stepped in to help with her three boys. I was starting to get anxious and scared. Watching my sister made me believe that motherhood may be more than I bargained for, but I knew I had Harold to help me and he still worked to take really good care of me. He paid all of the bills for us and would massage my legs and ankles after a long day of work. I was really in love with him but still proceeded in our relationship with caution only because we weren't married. He often talked about the type of father he wanted to be and I would daydream about us taking walks by the lake or playing at the park on a bright sunny day with our baby. If he loved the baby as much as he said he loved me, I felt that our family would last forever.

A lot of the guys in his Army unit would tease him about being a homebody or being tied down so about once a week he would hang out after work on the Army base or at his friend's house where we met. I didn't mind him going out as long as he respected the fact that he was in a relationship. One weekend Harold and his boys were getting away to Nasper City, which was about forty-five minutes away. I decided to stay with my sister just in case the baby decided to come earlier than planned. Angie and I talked about old times and some of my fears about motherhood. She shared some of her experiences about delivery, breastfeeding, and sleepless nights and none of these scared me, I was ready!

When Harold came back home I was there waiting for him with dinner and a nice warm bath. While he was in the tub, I started sorting clothes to do a couple of loads of laundry before it got too late. I always sort the clothes at the house before walking a half block to our laundry room past the other apartments in our complex. Harold took most of his clothes to the cleaners to be washed and pressed, but since he wasn't going to the cleaners until next week I added a few of his jeans and other items with mine. I was almost done turning all the shirts and socks inside out, sorting and taking any forgotten items from our pockets. I picked up Harold's pants from his overnight bag that he had taken with him over the weekend, as I pulled items from his pockets- gum, cigarettes, receipts, and some change. I laid it all on the coffee table. I let Harold know that I was heading to the laundry room but didn't leave until I looked through the papers that I had taken from his pocket. There was almost a play-by-play account of his overnight festivities just from his receipts. They ate at Krystal's, bought liquor and cigarettes, patronized two clubs that had valet parking and stayed at the Red Roof Inn. Wait!!!! They were supposed to stay at a friend's house because I had talked to the friend's wife; I wonder why things had changed. I needed to ask Harold because he never mentioned that they had changed their plans. I slowly walked into the bathroom where he comfortably soaked with his eyes closed as only candles lit the room. I thought about how I would approach him and quickly went over my line of questioning in my head. I softly called his name so I wouldn't startle him but he jumped anyway. "Harold how was your weekend with the boys?" "It was okay," he said, same as usual, drinking, smoking, and clubbing. "Did anything change in your plans that you want to share with me?" I was trying to be as calm as possible as I leaned my back against the sink with my arms folded on top of my big belly. "No, nothing changed- what's up Faith, what's with the line of questioning- did you miss big daddy that much that you want a play-by-play account of the weekend?" "No, I want to know why big daddy stayed at the Red Roof Inn and with whom?" Harold sat straight up in the tub and almost knocked over a candle that sat on the edge of the large tub. "What are you talking about, Faith?" "As I cleared out your pockets to do laundry, I found a hotel receipt; you were supposed to spend the night at a friend's house so why did you need to get a room?" "Let me see that!" He reached for the receipt and dripped water all over the floor. I just moved away and walked out of the bathroom. I could hear him fumbling around trying to get out of the tub. Finally he appeared in our bedroom dripping wet and standing butt naked in the doorway. "Well sir, it seems that you have some explaining to do, I'm listening!" "Faith, I'm sorry." He lowered his head while walking towards me. My heart was beating fast as he tried to force the crumpled receipt from my clinched fist that I wanted to use to punch him. I knew in my heart this receipt was not just from a room where him and his boys stayed while in Nasper City because now he was trying to pull me towards the bed to listen to his story. I was so upset I was shaking and my baby was turning flips in my stomach. I couldn't even look at him as he told me about some girl he made arrangements to meet up there. He explained that he did go out with the guys, but she met him at the room later and they spent the night together. I thought I was going to faint. It felt like the baby was cutting off my air supply as I shifted from side to side trying to relax my body so the baby would calm down. I looked into his eyes and simply asked "Why? What have I done wrong?" I thought I was doing everything to keep him happy, even having sex when it was quite uncomfortable. I jumped up and rushed into the bathroom with tears rolling down my face. I looked at myself in our large mirror that covered the wall over the sink and thought I could see why he would want someone else. I was a far cry from the girl he had met with a small waist and frame, hair put together, and dressed in fitted clothes to expose my cinched waist. I guess I got too comfortable too quick and this is where it got me. I sat on the toilet seat with my face in my hands feeling betrayed and let down. But mostly thinking what the next steps would be. I was all ready to re-enter our bedroom with demands of what he better do to keep me, but I quickly thought what if he doesn't want to keep me? What if she is who he wants? What if... he was planning to leave the baby and me? What would I do?

I stood at the bathroom door with my hand on the knob trying to prepare myself for whatever he would say, knowing that I had more than me to be concerned about at this point and would have to be the strong lady my dad had raised me to be, always ready and able to take care of myself. When I opened the door, he was standing there looking straight into my eyes saying it would never happen again, he didn't love her at all, and that he just let his hormones get the best of him, speaking almost in a whisper. I just brushed past him and went to lie in the bed. I could feel him standing near the bed just looking at me before he turned and walked to the living room. I must have cried myself to sleep, but when I got up a couple of hours later to put my gown on, I crept into the living room to see if he had left the house. He was just balled up on the couch still naked from getting out of the tub. I walked over, threw a blanket on him and returned to bed. I wanted to grab the broomstick and strike him as hard as his words had struck my heart but it wouldn't do any good, the damage was done and I had to figure out a way to deal with it.

Things around our house were a little tense. I was having a hard time trusting that he was where he said he would be or doing what he said he would be doing, but I was trying to make the best of it because the baby was due any day. He was coming straight home each day and even home for lunch on days I didn't have to work, but I was now left to contemplate details about the female he had cheated with. Did she work with him? How had he met her? Was it over? He apologized each day and assured me that it wouldn't happen again, but I still felt alone. He never told me any particulars about the female and honestly I was trying to wipe the whole ordeal into the back of my mind. Trying to get things ready for the baby was keeping me occupied along with still working both of my jobs in the mall. I would be really tired, but my managers were really good about allowing me to only sit and work the register; especially on days when I worked at both places. It was the Christmas season so they really needed me, plus I had promised myself that I would work up until the baby came and even comprised a plan with my co-workers in case I was at work when the action started.

I was long overdue for a day off and feeling a little uncomfortable so I called off work just to get some rest, but when I woke up I felt a burst of energy. I started thinking that maybe I just needed a couple of extra hours of rest and could have been okay to go to work. I put the baby's mint green linen on the bed, filled the diaper stacker and hung it on the end of the bed. I cleaned our whole little apartment from front to back, vacuuming, mopping, wiping things down, and even threw away some expired items from our cabinets and organized them. I was on a roll when Harold came home and said, "What's gotten into you?" I was just excited to have gotten so much done and even made time to have his dinner and bath ready for him when he got home from work. He had been coming home each day at the exact same time and today was no different. As we sat down to dinner and discussed our day, my back started to hurt badly. Harold started scolding me saying that maybe I had moved around too much that day, and maybe I had, but it was worth it to have a spotless house. I put my feet up into the chair across from me as we continued with our dinner, but shortly after another pain hit. This time it was accompanied by tightness in my stomach. I didn't say anything to Harold, but about ten minutes later when it happened again, I could tell by the way he was looking at me that he thought something was wrong. I had Braxton Hicks before which were false labor pains that were uncomfortable, but this time it hurt badly. I tried to breathe through the pains like I had been taught in our child birthing classes, but the tears starting to fill my eyes and I got scared. They were now coming about every eight minutes and I had moved from the table to the couch hoping that if I stretched my body out the pain would subside... but it didn't. I told Harold to call my sister Angie and he did. He was red in the face and looked so scared, but my sister tried to calm him down by telling him ways to make me more comfortable. He rubbed my back and my feet and even ran me some bath water, which I thought would help relieve the pain. Going from one room to the other lasted for hours until I just couldn't take it anymore and we left for the hospital at about four in the morning. I held onto the car door handle, squeezing anytime I had a pain. I wanted to scream, but had heard that it wouldn't do anything to make the pain stop so why waste energy I knew I would need later. It felt like Harold went the scenic route to the hospital and took every curve in town. I fussed the whole time feeling that he wasn't being considerate at all the pain I was enduring. When I got to the hospital, the doctor checked me. She told me I was only 2 centimeters dilated and could still have a long time before there was a baby. Harold and I walked the halls of the hospital for hours, stopping for me to catch my breath between contractions, while Harold allowed me to lay my head on his chest and rock through the pain. He called Angie every hour and she finally told him when she got her boys off to daycare that she would head to the hospital. When she finally arrived Harold left to go get coffee and some fresh air. Angie told me about all the crazy conversations she had with him each time he called her from the house and hospital. The baby seemed like it did not want to make an entrance into the world that day, but I didn't know how much more I could take. I was so tired I went back to my room to try and get some rest. They gave me an epidural that relieved the pain and allowed me to close my eyes for a couple of hours. When I woke up, I was feeling pressure and explained to the doctor that I was feeling very uncomfortable. When the doctor checked to see how I was progressing using her fingers to measure my cervix, a gush of water filled my bed and I just looked at her with big wide eyes. She smiled and said, "There's no turning back now, you are almost ready to push." Angie went to get Harold who was standing outside talking to a couple of our friends that just arrived to support us. At that point I was overcome with fear and I couldn't stop shaking. Not realizing this process had taken most of the day, my sister had to leave to pick up her boys, which meant that Harold would be on his own until she got back. As soon as she left the doctor came and I started to push. Harold was trying very hard to support me with words of encouragement while holding my left leg to assist me in my pushing. The nurse held my right leg and counted through the pushing, but I was so tired. I felt like there would be no way to have enough energy to push my baby out but I had to, I had no other choice. I lay there watching the doctor put on her green outfit with gloves and a mask. She laid out several white pads at the end of my bed and told me to slide down. She checked me again and said, "The head is crowning, we are ready. When I say push, put your chin to your chest and bare down, push from your bottom not your face" she instructed. I did just that and in no time felt a burning sensation. I was determined to deliver my baby as quickly as possible because I was so tired. I was pushing so well the doctor had to tell me to wait so they could prepare for my bundle of joy to enter the world. On the next push, he plopped out into the world. My beautiful baby boy was born at 6:00pm, weighing 7lbs. and 14oz. I was in love!!!

Chapter 8

After the baby came home, Harold and I gave him all of our attention. I took care of him while Harold was at work, but when he came home he jumped right into action as a proud papa. We named our son Jacobi; a name that was suggested to us by my middle sister Tonji in Chicago, and I think it fit him quite well. During delivery, his little collarbone was broken, but the doctor assured us that it was something that happened often and would heal itself in only a few weeks. We just had to handle him with extra care when dressing and undressing him but other than that he was perfect. Too bad I couldn't say the same for our relationship; I forgave Harold for cheating on me but could not forget about it. Even though I was distracted with our new baby, my trust was gone, but I was willing to try and allow him to work at earning it back for Jacobi's sake. When Jacobi was about eight weeks old I took a trip to Chicago so that my family could meet the new addition to our family. I stayed there only four days because I was so worried about

Harold cheating on me again that I couldn't enjoy my family. When it was time to go home, I asked Harold to take the six-hour drive to come and pick us up to take us back to Tennessee, and he did. Things seemed to fall apart only a few months after my visit to Chicago. We argued a lot, said things that were mean and hurtful, and finally agreed that this relationship might not be the best situation to raise our son in. When Jacobi was eight months old, I moved back in with Angie who had recently also gone through a separation from her husband. We pulled together for the sake of our boys and went on taking care of business like we knew we had to. Harold still helped and supported me with Jacobi. He and I even started to become friends again, but knew that we would never again be in a romantic relationship and I was okay with that. When I thought about him cheating while I was carrying his son, working two jobs, and playing wife, I was just too angry to totally forgive and that wasn't fair to either one of us. Right after Jacobi's first birthday Harold got out of the Army and moved to Las

Vegas to live with his mom, two sisters, and little brother. It was heartbreaking to not have him for the day-to-day help with Jacobi, but he made up for it by sending money faithfully and coming to visit every few months. Jacobi always bounced around like a wind-up toy every time he was with his dad.

That next year seemed to go by so quick. Working and taking care of Jacobi were my primary responsibilities. Watching him take his first steps, laugh, and even talk for the first time would be things I would never forget. My social life was non-existent but I wouldn't change creating memories and bonding with my baby boy for anything. When Harold came to town, he always brought us arms full of gifts and was ready to spend as much time with Jacobi as he could before returning back to his new life in Las Vegas. I would often talk to his mom to keep her updated on her grandson's growth and she would compare him to how Harold was growing up which I thought was hilarious. Harold had absolutely created a mini-me for himself. Jacobi was short and plump, with braids, and his brown skin was the exact tone of his dad's. Harold enjoyed buying Jacobi the most stylish clothes and name brand shoes, which always made him look like a little man. Within the next few weeks Harold would be traveling to Tennessee to take Jacobi to visit with him for the summer. This would be my first time away from my baby for an extended amount of time and the first time Jacobi was flying. I was very concerned that no one would look after my baby like me and as the visit got closer I started to have some reservations. Despite my better judgment, I agreed to let my baby travel with his dad as was only fair since I got a chance daily to watch Jacobi grow and I'm sure Harold's family would enjoy quality time with the newest member of their family.

On the day they were to leave I found myself so emotional, crying a lot but most of the tears came when I hugged and kissed my baby in the back seat of his dad's rental car as they headed to the airport for their long flight. I stared into his big round eyes wanting instantly to unstrap him and change my mind. But I wouldn't dare refuse a father's precious bonding time with his son.

While Jacobi was in Las Vegas, I planned to move into an apartment so that my sister and I could have our own space. Two weeks before Jacobi left for Las Vegas, I reached out to the management company of the apartments Harold and I previously lived in and found out they had some available apartments that I could move into right away. Jacobi and I didn't have much outside of clothes so I would just use my sister's car to move. I spoke to Jacobi everyday, but Harold was never really home with him. Jacobi was spending a lot of time with his grandmother, uncle, and aunts while Harold was doing God knows what in the streets. My summer days were so methodical; get up, go to work, come home, eat dinner, shower, go to bed. Start over the next day with the same routine. Nothing exciting was happening in my life at this time and now it was even worse because I was missing my baby boy. When I came home from work this particular day, I saw on my caller I.D. that my son's grandmother had tried calling me several times. "What does she want?" I thought frowning while holding the phone in my hand. This is my summer to myself. If she is not calling to tell me that my son has done an extraordinary feat, I don't want to talk. Usually if Harold wanted to contact me, he would page me or call from his cell phone. When I called back to her house, I actually asked if Harold was there. His mom gave a long pause and then in a slow and quiet tone said, "Harold was killed today." All I could do was yell, "Oh my God!" in a gut-wrenching voice that made my insides feel like my abdominal muscles were being squeezed together. Time froze and the phone seemed so heavy in my hand, my eyes focused on the window right in front of me. Gazed beyond the sheer curtains, behind the glass into the heart of the cruel world that just made me a single mother who for a lifetime would have to explain to a boy why his father wasn't just a phone call away ready to support him at games or special events. I slid from the bed where I was sitting to the floor in slow motion while holding the phone in my hand. I started to cry hysterically and she was doing the same on her end. Screaming through my many questions, she tried explaining to me what happened but to this day I don't remember much of what she said. I instantly started to mourn for all of those times Jacobi and I would have to take on things alone, forever missing the third piece to our puzzle. After I calmed down and stopped crying frantically, I asked if Jacobi, my son, was with his dad at the time and begged her to please tell me my baby was okay. She told me that he was okay, but that they were all being placed under police protection because his aunt was an eyewitness. The people who murdered Harold lured him to an apartment by holding a gun to his sister and making her call him. When he got there and got out the car, they met him, robbed him, shot him in the stomach, and ran away. He died on the scene with his sister watching through a window too afraid to exit to help her brother, not knowing if they were coming back for her. Under the circumstances, she did all she could. She called the police and prayed they would request an ambulance. Harold lay dead on the sun-baked street in Las Vegas for three hours before the investigation was over and was then moved to the coroner for a full autopsy. Three days passed and we met in Texas for the funeral, where Jacobi's grandfather and extended family live. Jacobi and I were reunited. I stood outside of the funeral home hugging my baby so tight that time stood still while I looked into the eyes of my son. With eyes just like his dad, this is all I would ever have left of Harold, along with the memories we shared. I'm sure this will be the last time he will see this side of his family. The only real thing that kept us connected was Harold.

I was so thankful for my family and friends for their support while I went through a deep depression trying to get my life together after Harold's death. The unit he worked for raised money to help me drive to Texas for his funeral services and even allowed the friends that he had lived with to escort me on behalf of the United States Army. They also presented his mom with the United States flag at the cemetery during the burial.

Chapter 9

I had to pull myself together for Jacobi and me. I had just begun a new job and was still working to get our apartment in order by unpacking and decorating to make it our own. Life was slowly getting back on track and I even got the opportunity to enroll Jacobi at the daycare center I now worked at. My time of working two jobs had come to an end because I didn't want to spend that much time away from Jacobi and I needed a set schedule. This job was my best option. It allowed me the opportunity to spend the day watching Jacobi learn new things and gave me bonding time with him in the evenings. I was so glad to be heading home from another day of full-time work at the daycare. I work every day with two-year-olds crying, coloring, and potty training. Driving home is always my time to unwind and reflect on my life or certain situations. Sometimes I wonder back to happy times but mostly feel sorry for myself because where I am in life is not where I would like to be. Years ago I actually had goals but due to a few setbacks, I now feel that those ambitions are far-fetched. I drove into my apartment complex and gathered my thoughts as I sat and waited on my friend Sandra to stop by. She called me the night before and said she would be in our area and wanted to see Jacobi. Sandra and I had met when I worked at the mall. She also worked in a store there and we connected because we were pregnant at the same time. Her gorgeous daughter had come two weeks before Jacobi and we allowed them to play together anytime we had some free time.

I snapped out of my thoughts when I noticed a guy standing in the doorway of the apartment next door to mine. Pretty Mill's Apartments is where I moved after living at my sister's house for a while. I chose this part of town because it was fairly safe when I lived here before and had a main road right off the apartments that led to many stores and restaurants. When I come home each day with my son following close holding my hand, I am very proud to finally be on my own for the first time in my life. I have lived in these apartments for a little while now, but only recently have we had late night noise and constant traffic. Last month some new people moved in right next door to me and I am not happy with them right now and really wish they would go back where they came from... I've seen this guy outside a few other times before but we never spoke to one another.

As I make eye contact with the noisy neighbor, my friend, Sandra, pulls up with her baby girl. When Jacobi sees them, he starts wailing his arms, smiling big at me, and yelling "mommy, mommy!" When we got out of our cars, I swept Jacobi up into my arms and kissed his pudgy little cheeks before passing him to Sandra who had her arms wide open reaching for him. Sandra tells me all about her day at the sister daycare of the daycare I work for. We swap stories of painting kids, crazy mamas, and mess-starting staff. While we are talking, the guy from next door just stands there, watching us while holding a glass, as if he had a front row seat to an intriguing movie. I guess Sandra noticed also and stated that she knew him. "Hey Thomas, how are you?" she says as she speaks to the gentleman next door. She must have caught him off guard because he has a big cheesy grin on his face and proceeds to walk towards where we are standing. "Hey girl," Thomas practically yelled. "I thought that was you!" What's up and how are your brothers?" Sandra asked. Thomas began to tell her that his younger brothers were doing well and his older brother was still working hard. Sandra listened attentively only nodding her head because she couldn't get a word in at all. While they reminisced over the past, I noticed my son had begun whining and reaching for me so I shifted over and started playing with him. Sandra looked over and says, "Faith, come here."

I walk over with a noticeable frown on my face and say, "What's up?" With Mr. Smiley actually standing too close, she then says, "This is Thomas, an old friend of my brothers." During our introduction, I can't help but notice that he is wearing blue jean shorts with boots, smells like he has drowned himself in cologne, and has not shaven for a couple of days. He stares and then reaches out his hand to shake mine. "Hello Ms. Lady," I say "hello" but really want to ask if they can keep their partying down because my son does like to sleep at night and I have to go to work in the mornings. To this day, I will never forget that grin, his smile reminded me of the big bad wolf when he had Little Red Riding Hood trapped and was about to pounce on her. He tells Sandra to be sure to tell her brothers he said hello as he turns to leave and says "goodbye".

Sandra looks at me and starts to give me the low-down on his family. He has a woman that he has been dating off and on for years and has three children. He has three brothers, two younger and one older. The older brother has special needs and works as a bouncer at the nightclubs that we hang out at. She thinks it is so funny that he wanted her to introduce him to me because she says his woman is crazy. Sandra starts to tell me a story in her often-animated way about a time when Thomas was hanging out at a friend's house with her brothers.

This woman of his came by and drove over the fence in the front of their house because he wouldn't come out. She was screaming, "You better not be in there with another woman. Get your butt out here now! NOW, I mean it!!" He didn't move. The homeowner ended up calling the police. All I could say is "WOW!" Barely able to speak, I was laughing hysterically. "Now that chick is psycho!" Sandra and I hugged briefly and said our goodbyes. She got in her car to leave while Jacobi and I went into our apartment.

Chapter 10

More partying and loud music go on next door. At least now when I pull into the parking lot and Thomas is outside, he yells to someone named Raymond, to turn the music down like he is trying to earn brownie points with me or something. Coming home now just makes my stomach turn, the loud beats of the latest music is annoying when I have worked all day and just want to come home and relax. Each day as I get out of my car to check my mail, I can feel him staring long and hard at me like he knows what time I arrive and is waiting on me to come down the street, creepy. I find it hard to understand what he is looking for when I notice him out of my peripheral vision- I am only wearing some slacks, a button-up shirt, and flats for comfort while playing with toddlers all day, but he is staring like I have on a short skirt, low-cut top and heels. It's almost spooky, but I still wave back when he waves at me after I catch him staring. My sister, Angie, is coming over later so that we can go out. I am very excited because I hardly ever get a chance to go out. When we do, it's a blast. Sandra offered to pick Jacobi up and take him home with her to spend the night and play with Destiny, her daughter. I took advantage of having a babysitter and looked forward to a good time, something I haven't had in a very long time.

My sister Angie is still serving in the United States Army. She's now enjoying her life as a single woman. After years of being unhappy in her marriage, she and her husband decided to divorce. When Angie arrives to my apartment she beats on the door with the sides of her closed fist like someone is chasing her. She is practically screaming when I let her in because old school slow jams were blaring from the neighbor's apartment. "Who lives next door? My God is that where the party is? Are they single because there are guys everywhere out there?" I'm like, "Dang crazy! All I know is one is named Thomas, but I don't know anyone else." We had talked about possible clubs we wanted to drop by that night but our minds weren't made up. We touched up our simple makeup of eyeliner and lip-gloss, grabbed our purses, and headed out the door to her car. Before we can take off though, five guys trying to talk to us bombarded our car. I guess they saw my sister on her way in and liked what they saw! Thomas introduces himself to my sister. The next guy steps up and says he is Raymond, Thomas' little brother. The other guys introduce themselves one by one also; Dex, Sidney, and Ryan. Thomas is now at my window asking where we are going. I tell him Club Dynamic, hoping they were going somewhere else but unfortunately he replies, "Us too! We'll see you there. Save me a dance." As my sister drives off, I looked at her and said, "Maybe we should go somewhere else. They were already drinking and seemed off the chain!" Angie figured they should be even more off the chain at the club and it would be fun.

When we got to the club, it was jumping. They were playing a fast beat hip-hop song so the dance floor was packed. Other people were walking around with their drinks and bopping to the music. Females were walking around half-dressed with shirts and dresses that barely covered their cleavage and painted-on jeans and skirts. Dudes salivated while trying to figure out which one they would attempt to take home with them. As soon as we walked in, we saw Thomas and his crew standing close to the bar. I told my sister that they had spotted us but because of the loud music she was saying, "What? What?" I just said, "Forget it, here comes that Thomas guy." He was wearing a long-sleeve, tan plaid shirt opened with a t-shirt underneath, jeans, and timberland boots. He looked nice but just wasn't my type. He came over and asked me to dance while his friend that he called "Black" grabbed my sister and took her to the dance floor. I told him I wouldn't dance with him because our body parts didn't match up. He was too tall for me and would have to wait on a faster song. He told me he didn't dance too much faster than that so I danced with him. All night, Thomas and his friends kept finding my sister and me but we didn't dance with them again. I was looking at their entire crew wondering who would drive them home because they were all getting blasted. Angie and I did have a good time at the club. On our way home, we were discussing how many drinks they had bought for us. Good thing we were only having juice and pop.

The next day when I ran into Raymond outside of the apartments, he asked if we had a good time the night before. He said they had a good time and invited us to go out with them again that night. I passed. One night with strangers was enough.

Angie came over and brought her two youngest boys with her. We sat outside of my apartment and drank coolers while the kids played. As it started to get dark, Thomas and Raymond's apartment started to fill up. Soon they piled into cars with their brown bags and left. My sister started to question what I knew about them. I had no information at all. Although I felt like Thomas was always watching me, I never really paid very much attention to him.

The next day I sat outside of my apartment with my son just enjoying the March weather. It was very nice for that time of year. The weather was warm with just a light wind that felt cool to the side of my face. I heard the door of my neighbor's apartment open. I said to myself, "Oh God." Thomas came out and over to me and said "Hello neighbor, how are you?" I said "Fine" but I never looked up at him. So he then came around and sat on my car in front of me, which is only a couple of feet from my door. He asked if I minded some company and of course I said I didn't mind. While my son played, we talked about our jobs, families, children, and futures. He shared with me that his mom was in the Army years ago, which is how they came to live in Tennessee. His family was originally from Alabama and their mom raised him and his brothers. She allowed them to experience many things like drinking and smoking during their teenage years reasoning that if they did it with her they wouldn't sneak and do it in the streets. Thomas appeared to be a person with good sense. But that could have been fake and if it was, he had me fooled. After a couple hours of conversation, I told him I wanted to head inside, feed my son, and put him to bed. He asked if I would be back out later and I simply replied "maybe". He said, "Well I know where to find you." Later on, we met back outside. It felt like we were both coming out of our apartments at the exact same time. We both talked about where we were from and what our lives were like in Tennessee. We chatted more about our families, our jobs, and made small talk about how we like to spend our free time. By this time more hours had passed and it was 11:00 pm. Both of us were yawning and admitted we were tired and had to get up for work the next day. It had been a while since I had hung out or just had a long conversation with a guy and was still thinking about him when I went into the house.

A couple more weeks passed. Thomas and I would sit and talk into the wee hours of the night. We both had a strong connection with our families and talked about traditions that had been established as we grew up. I was often intrigued by stories he would share about him helping his mom, Janet, take care of his brothers by doing the shopping, cooking, and ironing when she had to be away because of her commitments in the Army.

On occasion, I would also talk to a girl named Tanya who would come over and see Raymond. She was a thin, dark-skinned girl with really long hair who seemed cool but didn't talk much. She said her and Raymond had just started to see each other only a few weeks before we met. I found it funny that she had a baby that looked only to be a few weeks old and she spent a lot of time next door and not at home. I guess stranger things could happen. She always had her little baby with her whenever she came to visit so I guess she is a mom whose baby is an important part of her life and Raymond was becoming just as important to her. After Thomas and I hung out together a few more times, he explained that he and his ex-girlfriend had been together off and on for the last ten years. This time, he said, it was over for good because he just couldn't take her anymore. He also shared with me that he worked from five in the morning to one in the afternoon. Every time there was partying at his house, he didn't like it. I jokingly said, I definitely understood and if he needed to get some rest and couldn't at his house, he could sleep on my couch. He laughed and said he would keep that in mind.

Chapter 11

Thomas and I became really good friends and hung out at my apartment all the time watching movies and just talking when we weren't busy working. It was great to have the company of a man again but it was so funny for me to be spending so much time with someone who I said was not my type. Normally the guys I dated were a little more fashion savvy, not party animals, and definitely not fresh out of a long-term relationship.

When Thomas would come over to watch movies we would always have to watch them in my bedroom which sometimes made things very inconvenient, but that was the only place I had a television and VCR. He would always laugh at me because Jacobi and I would be on my bed, while he had to sit in a chair next to my bed. I told him that no man was allowed to be in my bed except my son, but the truth was that I was so horny there is no telling what would happen if he sat that close to me, especially in my bed and if my son wasn't there. I could see us watching a romantic movie and quickly becoming its characters. Me pulling and tugging at his clothes as he kissed my neck. He held me tight with both arms as our bodies did a slow and sensual dance.

Days went on with us taking Jacobi to the park and just spending time together, when one night at about eleven o'clock there was a knock on my door. I was just lying in my bed watching television while Jacobi was fast asleep. When I looked out of the blinds and saw Thomas standing there I smiled but knew I couldn't hang out because I had to go to work the next day. I opened the door and could instantly tell he had been drinking because I could smell liquor and his eyes were red but he wasn't drunk. I asked what he was doing at my door that time of night. He looked at me with a cheetah grin and said, "I am here to take you up on your offer of sleeping on your couch. We have company again." I allowed him to come in and gave him a blanket. Later on when I went to the washroom, I peeked in to make sure everything was okay with him and found myself just staring his way in the dark until I heard him say, "Is everything okay, Faith?" All I could say was, "yeah," because not only was I embarrassed for acting like a stalker but he scared the daylights out of me. I got back in the bed and didn't wake back up until four a.m. At that time he was leaving for work, came in my room, said a gracious "thank you" and kissed me on my cheek. The next day I called Angie to tell her Thomas had spent the night with me and she went crazy. She yelled, "How well do you know him girl?" I told her that he slept on the couch and that it was very innocent to calm her down.

A couple of days later Thomas caught me coming home from work again and asked if he could come over and watch a movie, but this time I told him I had a better idea and I would see him at 7:30pm. After he walked away from the door, I sprang into action straightening up the house, starting dinner, and giving Jacobi his bath. At exactly 7:30pm, Thomas was at the door and I had a nice dinner waiting for us. I fed Jacobi a little early, allowed him extra playtime in the tub and put him in his toddler bed with one of his favorite LONG movies. Thomas and I sat down at the dining room table sitting directly across from each other where eye contact was inevitable. We enjoyed extra cheesy homemade lasagna, tossed salad, and garlic bread. I set the table with a red tablecloth and my best black dishes. He said it was the best dinner he'd had in a long time and made sure he said "thank you" several times that evening. We sat at the table talking about everything under the sun and enjoying each other's company. Thomas gave me the third-degree about Jacobi's dad, my family, and asked if I ever planned to return to Chicago. As we were wrapping up dinner, we heard loud banging on a door and then a car screech out of our apartment complex.

After speculating about how crazy that person must be, we were interrupted by a loud knock on my door. I went and answered it; it was his brother Raymond telling him he needed to see him right away. Thomas kept asking him, "What's up?"

Finally, before I could close and lock the door behind Thomas, I heard Raymond say that Thomas' ex -girlfriend had come and dropped his three children off to him and said she had somewhere to go. Thomas said, "What? I know she didn't. What else did she say?" Raymond said, "She didn't say much more, she just left." At 10:30, Thomas called me and asked if he could come back over, of course I said "yes." When he came back he explained that she gets mad when she calls for him and Raymond says he doesn't know where he is. So she was trying to inconvenience both of them by just dropping the children off. But it was no big deal because she didn't realize he was just next door and the kids loved spending any time they could with him or their uncle. The children had laid down and were sound asleep before he crept back over to my apartment, but I told him I didn't want him to stay long that night because I didn't want any problems if she came back. I guess he felt guilty about our dinner being interrupted and felt the need to explain the situation with his ex and the kids. His kids were five, six, and eight-years-old and he told me that he does not go over to visit them a lot because of the grief that he has to take from her about them no longer being together after ten years. His explanation did not help the uneasiness I felt about the situation, but he said he understood. He fixed himself a to-go plate, gave me a kiss on the cheek, and went back next door.

Chapter 12

Jacobi was going away for the weekend with his Godmother, Danita. I was happy to be getting some alone time. I love my son more than anything but ME time was exactly what I needed. His Godmother and a friend of Harold's had been dating while I was pregnant with Jacobi. She and I became really good friends. Before I delivered Jacobi, we asked them to be Jacobi's Godparents and they accepted. Since then, they broke up and Harold's friend didn't keep in contact with me when he was stationed at another Army base. Danita loved Jacobi and allowed him to spend time with her when she was available. His Godmother met me at my apartment at 6:00pm Friday evening. She explained that she probably wouldn't bring him back until late Sunday evening. Jacobi grabbed his bag, blanket, and big stuffed Scooby Doo and almost knocked himself over as he yelled, "Bye, Bye, mommy." I gave him a big hug and kiss and told him to be good. I told Danita that I appreciated her so much for allowing me to have time to myself. I explained that I didn't know what I would do without her taking him every now and then.

When they left, I laid down to take a nap but was soon awakened by a knock at the door. I went to answer and looked through the blinds to see Thomas looking right back at me. He came inside and just stood in my living room and looked at me. He asked, "Did I see my little partner leave?" I said, "Yes, stalker!" He laughed at me and grabbed and hugged me. I didn't know what to do so I hugged him back. But that friendly hug turned into a tighter more affectionate hug, which slowly led to a sensual kiss. I was so aroused that I kissed him back so hard that he probably thought I was a freak. I pressed my body into him and held on for dear life, wanting that kiss to last forever. He stopped and said, "I hope that was okay with you?" All I could say was, "YESSSSS!" It was very awkward for the next few minutes. We soon started a conversation about who Jacobi left with and how long he would be gone.

Thomas hung out at my apartment a little while longer and watched a movie with me until I fell asleep. When I woke up the next morning, he was in the living room sprawled out on the couch like a little boy. Even though I was ready to get up and do my normal Saturday morning chores, I threw a blanket on him and then lay back in my bed a while longer. Thomas came in to let me know he was leaving and leaned down to give me a kiss goodbye. When he did, I think the kiss lasted much longer than we both expected .He started by running his hands across my shoulders and down the small of my back. It had been so long since I had been touched this way. Thomas caressed my body, every touch brought chills over me, as we made love. I felt like I was in heaven.

I didn't think things could get any better between us. We laid together for what seemed like the rest of the day, finally getting up, taking a shower, and going to grab something to eat.

Later on that evening, my sister and I got all jazzed up and headed to Club Dynamic. Thomas, Raymond, and his girlfriend met us there. We all had a few Long Island Ice Teas. We danced and had a good time all evening long. When we would sit back down, we would order another round of drinks, and then danced again. Angie finally said she was done drinking and wanted to sober up so we would get home safely. But that didn't matter to me, Thomas was buying and I was drinking, a lot. I felt myself going drink for drink with Thomas. This was not how much I normally drank but I was having a ball. Raymond and his girlfriend had other plans after the club so they left earlier than we did. My sister dropped Thomas and I off at my apartment. I was so drunk that all I could do was cry and hug the toilet. I threw up time after time and it felt like my insides were ripping apart. I explained to Thomas that I had never been that drunk in all my life. But before I could complete my sentence, I was back over the toilet. When I finally got off of the floor, I stood in the doorway of my bedroom and attempted to tell Thomas how horrible I was feeling. I told him that I had a good time and "TTTTTTTHHHHank Yoooouuuu." As I said it, I found myself falling face first across the room into my refrigerator as I slid down to the floor. Thomas came and picked me up while repeatedly asking me if I was okay. He carried me to my bed and then lay down next to me. I went to sleep with the room spinning and my head pounding. I woke up the next day so embarrassed. Thomas made me feel better about it by assuring me that the little fiasco would be kept between us. I got up realizing I was still fully dressed from the night before, went in the washroom to brush my teeth and wash my face. I stood for a moment just staring at myself in the mirror thanking God for keeping me safe and promising him to never drink that much again. When I entered back into the living room, Thomas stood and grabbed my hands. I looked up into his eyes and said, "thank you for taking care of me so well." He wrapped his arms around my neck pulling my face into his chest and said, "No problem." We talked about the events of the night before and I finally got the courage to ask him if he drank alcohol every day. He answered "yes, I like to have a few drinks each day when I come home from work, just to unwind." Knowing this made me feel a little uncomfortable because that sounded like an alcoholic to me. It appeared that he was able to manage himself. I had to remind myself that I drank every now and then also, so it wouldn't be right for me to pass judgment on him. But with me getting drunk in front of him might open up doors that I am not prepared for. Now, he probably thinks that I always get drunk and it will also be okay for him to get drunk when he is with me. Although that conversation was still lingering in my mind, we got up, said our goodbyes for the day, and I cleaned up my apartment.

Chapter 13

Everything seemed to be going well with my life. My relationship with Thomas was great and Jacobi liked him a lot so that made me feel good. One day some friends of mine at work were planning to hang out at another co-worker's house after work and they invited me. My friend also wanted me to braid her little girl's hair so I thought this would be the perfect time. After work, we headed to her house and the kids found toys to play with while the adults talked.

I started to braid the little girl's hair and my pager started to go off, it was Thomas calling from my house. I had given him a key a few days earlier so that if he wanted to come over late at night he wouldn't have to wake me up. The lady whose house I was at didn't have a phone so I couldn't call him back. He was being persistent, calling every fifteen minutes. I knew I wouldn't be much longer so I kept braiding and when I was finished, I headed to my apartment. When I got home, I could see the lights on so I knew he was there. I was anxious to see him and hoped he still wanted to see me; with the way he paged me I thought I would walk into a big surprise from him. Yeah, it was a surprise alright, but not what I anticipated. I walked in to explain, but when I got in he was staring at me like I was crazy. He was furious and had been drinking. His face looked disfigured, I was almost afraid of the wrinkles in his forehead that clearly made me believe that he was angry. I put Jacobi in my room in front of the TV and put on one of his favorite sing-along videos. Thomas repeatedly talked over me while I was trying to explain. He said he had been waiting on me to come home, but I wasn't aware of that. He started yelling and screaming, "WHY DIDN'T YOU ANSWER MY PAGE? WHAT HAD YOU SO OCCUPIED?" He wouldn't let me get a word in so I started to yell back because I had done nothing wrong. I didn't understand where all of this was coming from. He then picked up my pager off the table and threw it outside across the parking lot. It shattered into small pieces off the door of the apartment across from mine. I stepped to him, looked him in his eyes and asked why he had done that. He said, "Why do you need it? You don't respond to it." I was so shocked, appalled, and disappointed. I could not believe he was acting like this but he didn't stop. He paced back and forth inside and outside the apartment.

He came back into my apartment and looked up at the wall. He appeared to get more upset as he snatched the pictures of Harold, Jacobi's dad off the wall. He said, "I get tired of looking at him every time I am over here." He left, storming towards the garbage dumpsters in our apartment complex with the pictures shifting in his hand. I ran behind him screaming and begging for him to stop. I jumped on his back to try to stop him but nothing worked. He rolled me off of his back, I grabbed him around his legs pleading with him by telling him I promised to call him back next time, but it was too late. He swung his arm back like he was pitching at a major league baseball game. He threw the pictures in the dumpster, all I could do was scratch at his arms to try and stop him but I did not succeed. I heard the pictures crash at the bottom of the dumpster that seemed to echo through our whole complex. I jumped up throwing my body over the side of the open hole with my feet dangling in mid-air above the huge dumpster trying to see how far the pictures had fallen in as tears streamed down my face. I was quickly reminded that it had been trash day as the pictures and shattered glass lay at the bottom too far to be reached. There was no way for me to get the pictures so they were gone forever. I thought about climbing into the dumpster but knew that I would just be stuck because he wouldn't care enough to help me get out. I jumped down and ran past him heading back into my apartment, my heart thumped so hard I could feel it through my chest. I fell limp on the couch and buried my face into the armrest, I felt so helpless!

When he came into my apartment I demanded that he give my key back and for him to get out. He slammed the key on the coffee table, looked at me with a smirk of gratification on his face, and turned to walk away. Because I knew he was only next door, I locked up my apartment and left in my car with my son just to go for a ride hoping this would allow him time to cool down and go to sleep. We rode around for about an hour trying to give Thomas enough time to cool down before I came back home. I was really scared, this is not like anything I had ever experienced in my life, it was no better that Jacobi kept asking me why I was crying and saying, "Don't cry mommy." I just told him that I was okay and I promised to stop crying. But I guess Thomas hadn't calmed down because when I drove back into the apartment complex, I could clearly see that my door was opened. I left Jacobi in the car, went in and noticed that my door had been kicked off of the hinges. The splintered wood around the inside edges were exposed. The lock was broken and one nail was missing. I walked in the apartment slowly not knowing if he was somewhere inside waiting on me. I tiptoed through to my bedroom even stepped in the bathroom to slowly peek behind the shower curtain, but before I pulled it back I noticed that Thomas had written on my mirror with lipstick, "WHEN I CALL YOU, YOU BETTER ANSWER." I ran out the apartment, called the police, and sat back in the car with the doors locked waiting. By the time the police arrived, they beat on his apartment door but Thomas could not be found anywhere. They filed a report and helped me close the door and told me to lock the chain at the top, lock all windows, and stay clear of Thomas.

The next day while I was going to get my mail, Thomas approached me apologizing profusely. I stepped back, moving away from him. He tried to justify his actions by saying that he was worried about me not coming straight home from work. When he realized I was okay, it turned into anger. He promised to fix my door and agreed that it was a good idea that I had taken my key back. He admitted he felt that he had jumped into a new relationship with me too fast. Every day following the fight, I walked into my apartment looking up at the now empty wall where Harold's pictures use to hang, feeling a tug at my heart and emptiness in the pit of my stomach. I tried to figure out if I had given Thomas any reason to be so jealous and to treat me that way. I rationalized with my own feelings thinking I too probably would have been upset; maybe he was really worried about us. After about a week of not spending time with him, I finally gave in to his apologies and his begging for us to start over; we started to see each other again.

Chapter 14

Thomas and I got really close again but now every time he called I made sure I was available. We would go out to the club together every now and then, but I was starting to notice how jealous he would get when I danced with other men. One night while we were out, he accused me of grinding my booty on some guy. That was the furthest from the truth, what I was doing was turning my back to get away from the guy because he was getting too close to me and making me feel uncomfortable. When I came off the dance floor, I passed the table where Thomas had moved to sit with a few of his friends, but to my surprise he had a woman sitting in his lap. We made eye contact, but no words were exchanged. He then walked passed me and headed to the dance floor for a slow dance with the same girl. Holding her hand and keeping her close behind him, a small space on the edge of the floor was made for them. I just sat at my table furiously watching him pull her closer as their bodies moved in sync. She held him around his neck and he placed his hands in the small of her back with his fingertips resting on top of her butt. She was almost as tall as he was so their faces leaned side by side while their lips seemed to murmur things in each other's ears that I could not make out. The song seemed to last so long. I tried to look away, but curiosity drew me back to his disrespectful actions right in front of my eyes. When he came back past my table, I stood up to block his path and told him, "I am ready to go. If you are planning to ride with me, you better be behind me," he turned and told the girl he guessed he would see her next time. My head spun around quickly, she and I made eye contact as we left the club. As I drove, we argued all the way home and he said he only did that to make me jealous, but it didn't. It only embarrassed me because I had friends there too who also watched his little slow dance and later questioned me about us being a couple. Thomas and I argued more often than I would have ever imagined we would, but making up was great! I started to make myself believe that he only acted this way because he liked me a lot and drank all the time. Apparently, he was used to drama from when he was with his ex girlfriend but I wasn't up for all of that.

After the club incident I stopped going out with him as much but he still went. Sometimes I would allow him to drive my car so that I knew he wouldn't be stranded at a friend's house and he could come straight home after the club, but that thought quickly diminished. He would use my car and most of the time he wouldn't bring it back until the next day or just when he wanted to. I was always just so happy to see that both he and my car were safe that I would only stay mad for a little while.

Thomas was back staying at the apartment more frequently and it was fun having someone to come home to. Sometimes I was surprised by flowers and dinner or if Jacobi was going away, I sometimes got a naked surprise with fresh fruit on the side.

Valentine's Day was slowly approaching and by now we had been dating for a little under a year. We were happy and really enjoyed each other's company, well, most of the time. We were trying to figure out what we could do for Valentine's Day and I wanted our plans to include Jacobi because he was also the love of my life. The days leading up to Valentine's Day, Thomas kept walking around patting the pocket of his jacket. I said, "I guess that is my gift." I liked surprises so I didn't try to figure out what it was. On Valentine's Day, I received a big bouquet of red roses at my job. All of the women were envious of me and it made me feel proud to have a man who cared so much about me. Later that evening, the three of us had dinner at home by candlelight and it was very sweet. After Jacobi went to bed, we put a blanket on the floor and had strawberries and wine to close out our evening. As we sat there and talked, Thomas said that he almost forgot to give me my present. I told him that it was okay because the day had been wonderful already. But he still left the room and came back and sat me on the couch. He started his speech by saying, "I am sorry for anything I may have put you through since we have been together. I love you. I enjoy spending time with both you and Jacobi and I love you. I would like to spend the rest of my life making up for all of the stupid mistakes I made the last few months because I love you, so will you marry me because as you know I love you." He pulled out a beautiful ring. I was shocked and soon saw why they make people sit down before they propose. The ring was gold with a large diamond in the middle circled by twelve smaller diamonds. I put my right hand on my chest, not realizing I was mimicking someone who was about to have a heart attack. After he actually spoke the words "Will you marry me?" I said "yes" and pounced on him, grabbing him tightly around the neck almost forcing him to topple over. We capped off the night by making love right on the floor in the dim light of the soft lamp and the dark midnight sky.

Chapter 15

Jacobi was getting to be a big boy and was learning so much at the daycare. He was cutting, gluing, and trying to print. I was so proud of him. He was an active little boy; he enjoyed running and playing all the time so much that his teacher had to allow him movement breaks in order for him to stay on task during work time. At home things were changing too, Thomas and I felt that paying rent for two apartments when we really only spent time in one didn't make very much sense, so we started to look for a larger place that we could live in together. Our search didn't go on too long because Raymond and his girlfriend Tanya had already moved together in an apartment not far from where we were already living. We applied there for a two-bedroom with walk-in closets and a huge living room and were successful in getting it. As soon as they called to say we got the apartment, we started to pack. This wasn't a long or extensive process because the apartment we were moving out of was furnished so we had to buy our larger household items brand new. When we went shopping for furniture, I would be on cloud nine because it made me feel as though we were a real family, but sometimes it would be ruined by just stopping at the store and Thomas picking up a six-pack of beer. Anything at any time could set him off when he drank or it could just relax him. I liked it better on the more relaxing days. We decorated every room but had the most fun putting together a Mickey Mouse room for Jacobi. We found life-size pictures of Mickey Mouse to put on the walls and bought beautiful red, black, and white curtains to tie all of it together. The first couple of nights Jacobi was not feeling the new apartment and definitely not his new room so we allowed him to sleep with us. We were so proud of our new apartment that after we had it set up the way we liked it, we had friends and family over to help welcome us into our new home. To my surprise everything went well even though we had drinks, card playing, and domino games. Everyone remained on their best behavior, even Thomas. Later that night, we discussed how fortunate we were to have our new bigger apartment and fell asleep in each other's arms. When we woke up, we found Jacobi at the foot of our bed, balled up tight with only the corner flaps of our comforter covering his little legs. He had slid into our bed without us even noticing, but we carefully took him and put him back in his bed and covered him with the large face of Mickey Mouse resting on his back. When he woke up later, we told him that only babies sleep in the bed with adults and he is supposed to be a big boy now. After that we never had trouble with him trying to sleep with us again.

Chapter 16

Fourth of July holiday was right around the corner
and Angie was planning a big barbecue at her
house. I think I was more excited than she was
because our whole family was coming down from
Chicago and Thomas' mother was coming from
Alabama. We cleaned her house from front to back
and made sure everyone would have some place to
sleep. Thomas' mother was planning to stay at a
hotel and that was okay with us. His mother came
down earlier than we thought and showed up to
surprise us. I had spoken to her several times on the
phone and really looked forward to bonding more
with her and learning more about their family. She
had traveled many places during her military career,
but loved her time in Tennessee and decided to
make it home for her and her boys. Once upon a
time she had been married to a gentleman who
loved his wife, but his African culture dictated that
he support his family in a controlling manner. This
sometimes made him difficult to live with so they
divorced when the boys were still young. From

what I quickly noticed, she enjoyed drinking like her sons. She came in asking for a run to be made to the store to grab a couple of beers. Thinking back to some of the stories Thomas told me about his teenage years, I knew that drinking was a part of their family traditions. After getting acquainted, she wanted to go and visit Thomas' three children so she left to do that. I thought it was great that he would meet her later to also spend time with his children even if it took his mom coming down for him to do so. Later on, Thomas left to the hotel his mother was staying at; I was to meet them there later. Since there was a large pool near the lobby of where his mom was staying, his ex-girlfriend decided to bring the children there to have fun during their visit with their grandmother. Angie and I went to the grocery store to get the rest of the items needed for the cook out; plenty of ribs, chicken, hot dogs, and extras to complete side dishes. After we got home, I headed to the hotel to visit with Thomas' mom too.

When I got to the hotel I had a big surprise waiting for me; I entered the pool area where I was expecting to meet Thomas and was astonished to see his three children still in the swimming pool, and their mother sitting on the side drinking a beer. She and I had seen each other before when we went to his children's sporting events, but we were never formally introduced. His mom thought that it was her place to do the honors and even had us sitting at the same table for small talk. I was furious. I told his mom I wasn't staying long because I had a lot to do so I asked Thomas if he would walk me to my car. When we got outside I let him have it and all he could say was, "I had nothing to do with them being here. My mom invited them and she was here when I got here." I still needed to know if he thought it would be okay with me if he spent family time with his ex-girlfriend. I just couldn't understand why she had to be there or why he had to stay. But of course, to him I was overreacting and he put me in the car, closed the door hard, and said he would see me within the hour back at home. That hour turned into four hours and he ended up coming home sloppy drunk with his brothers practically carrying him in.

When the holiday came my family arrived safely and that evening Thomas' mother accompanied us to Angie's house so she could meet my family. We danced, drank, and ate until we were about to burst. Everyone was laughing and joking and having a good time while we lit fireworks and watched them explode. Later that evening everyone was talking about going to the club. I really had had enough fun and was just ready to go home and go to sleep, but of course Thomas wasn't. I expressed to him that "I don't want to go out," and he blew up. Our argument only ended when my father walked up on us and said, "That's enough," but I knew it wasn't over. Thomas' mom said, "You should know better not to try to talk to him right now, you know how he gets so you should just learn to be quiet when he drinks." All I could do was look at her and say to myself, "Well if that's the case I will hardly ever have the opportunity to speak, he drinks every day." We said our goodbyes and Angie thanked everyone for coming as we headed home. Thomas drove home at one hundred miles an hour and scared me to death. He refused to let me drive even though he had massive amounts to drink and was sure to be over the legal limit of alcohol. He yelled, "You embarrassed me! You are loose, and you always want attention!" I had no idea what he was talking about, but only said "okay." I figured my short answers only made him madder because even though he could barely make it up the stairs to our apartment, he insisted on going out even if he had to go alone. When we got in the apartment he started to scream all kinds of obscenities at me and I just kept telling him, "I don't know what you are talking about." I finally told him, "You are drunk and do not drive my car anymore tonight," and took the keys. Oh my God! What was I thinking when I made that bold move? He started shoving me and even picked me up and threw me across the room because I would not give my keys to him. I had a rug burn on my elbow and a bruise on my hip. I crawled past him, crying non-stop, trying to get to the phone to call my family, but he unplugged it and took the phone. No matter how much I cried and begged he wouldn't give it back. When I tried to leave the apartment, he stood in the way so I couldn't get past him, with his arms out to the sides bending down to look into my eyes like he was defending an NBA player. When I tried to push past him he flipped me around, threw me on the floor, pinned me down with my arms against my back and sat on top of me. With all of his weight on my ninety-eight pound body, I started to hyperventilate, begging him to let me go until I eventually passed out. When I gained consciousness, I just lay there and pretended to still be out. He just continued to walk past me to get dressed so he could leave with no remorse that something could actually be wrong with me. As I continued to lie there, I heard him get on the phone and tell Raymond, "I'm on my way to the club. Faith tried to keep me here but it didn't work. She wrestled with me to try to keep the keys and ended up passed out, but I really think she is awake. I bet if I put something in her mouth she will get up," he laughed with a Santa Claus chuckle. I just lay there sick to my stomach and glad that my nephews had asked if Jacobi could spend the night with them so he wasn't home. Finally, he stepped over me and continued with his plans of meeting others out at the club, despite the fact that I passed out and was laying on the floor; I never opened my eyes before he left, but that didn't stop him. Did he think so less of me to just leave me passed out or was he just that concerned with continuing to get another drink? These are things I pondered as I got up to pick up the pieces to this night that started so well but ended like so many others. I was so hurt that he often treated me with such little respect. When things were good, I saw so much potential in our relationship, but when they were bad it made me feel lifeless.

When Thomas came home early in the morning hours I had the top lock closed so he couldn't get in thinking that he would just go to his brother's house down the block to sleep. He didn't of course; he kicked the door in. When I heard him beating on the door I was afraid, but he had warned me last time about calling the police on him so I just prayed until I finally heard the door come crashing in. I got in the closet and hid hoping he would think I was gone but I think he was too drunk to make it to the back of the apartment and just crashed on the couch. When I started to stir a couple of hours later I realized I was still in the closet and thought now would be a good time to say a prayer. *"Father God in the name of Jesus, I first want to thank you for bringing me this far. I know it was only you. I need your help Lord, please deliver me from this person who I have connected myself with. Please take the need for alcohol from his mouth and the constant thought of it from his mind. Lord please give me the strength to leave, I need you. This prayer I ask in your name, Amen".* After I said the prayer, I must have fallen back asleep because I woke up to, "Baby, baby come and get in the bed." He towered over me trying to appear loving and apologetic, but I just said, "That's okay. I am ready to get up anyway to clean up and go pick up Jacobi."

Later that day as I drove to pick Jacobi up, I started to plan my escape in my head. I would save up enough money to pack up all of my things and move back to Chicago so that I could be closer to my family, friends, and for support. For the next couple of months, Thomas was so nice to me... he bought me things, cooked dinner, and watched Jacobi while I either read a book or just relaxed. This made me feel really bad about my continuous thoughts of leaving him. Maybe I should just take his mother's advice and not talk to him when he's drinking. He could be so sweet sometimes, but it wasn't often enough to endure his hurtful episodes. Time went on and we had small arguments about him drinking too much or staying out all night, but nothing as bad as the Fourth of July. Until one day, I was coming home from work and Thomas and Raymond were standing out in front of the apartments. They were chatting away with some females that I had never seen before. When I got out of the car he continued to talk to them as though he did not see me, so after I was settled into the house,

I sent Jacobi to ask him to come to the apartment. When he came we just talked about our day and I asked, "Who are those girls you were talking to?" He answered quick and just said, "Some new neighbors." I didn't even feel like arguing with him and it made no sense to get into it over what was probably something innocent. We started doing our normal chores for the evening like dinner, ironing, and showers to prepare for the next day. No more was mentioned about the girls.

It was Saturday and all Thomas talked about was this party he was going to with Raymond. He assured me he wouldn't be gone all night because it was a house party being thrown in one of the apartments in our complex. Thomas was so nice all day, he took Jacobi and I to walk by the water, to lunch, and then by Angie's house just to hang out for a while. We had such a beautiful day I thought he would be compelled to stay home with us that night. NOT!!! Later that night, as he started to get dressed I asked, "What are you doing?" He looked at me and said, "Getting ready for the little house party. Oh! You wanna come?" I just looked at him because he knows that I had no one to watch Jacobi and he was halfway dressed and ready to leave. At about eleven o'clock I talked to Angie and she told me to come over to her house and hang out because they weren't doing anything but watching a couple of movies that she rented. I thought that would be great so I left Thomas a note in case he came back before I did. I got Jacobi ready and we headed out. As I was driving out of the apartments I saw a lot of people hanging out so I slowed down to see if I saw Thomas or Raymond to let them know I was leaving. I drove a little further and saw Thomas walking and holding a girl's hand. As they stopped he was right in her face, close enough to kiss, talking to her. When I pulled up next to them I put the car in Park and told Jacobi to stay in his car seat because I would be right back. I opened the car door, stepped out, and approached Thomas and the young lady. I said, "Hello, how are you? I am Thomas' fiancée. Nice to meet you...your name is?" I said as I reached out to shake her hand. She looked at him and said, "Oh, I thought you were just his roommate...my fault." She never extended her hand back to me, with this look of "OH WELL!" on her face. All I could do was look at him as he started to explain that they were just heading to the store. I said, "HOLDING HANDS, what's up with that?" He replied, "Oh nothing. Tracey, I will talk to you later. Can you tell my brother I said I am going home?" We got in the car and headed back home and had a big argument because he again said I overreacted. All I could think was, I can't take this anymore. I told him to leave and never come back. He responded by saying he was tired of me putting him out and this time he was gone and he was not coming back. He packed big plastic bags full of his clothes and then packed a Ziploc bag with his toiletries. I just sat and watched him not saying a word. When he left, he only took one bag with him and said since he was walking he would be back later for the other ones. He stood at the door, staring at me and asked "Are you sure this is what you want?" I dropped my head, looked down at the floor and allowed the silence to fill the room. The next sound I heard was the plastic bag rustling and the door shutting. After he left, I felt really bad, but only shortly because I know he is either back at that party or at his brother's place, but he definitely won't be staying in the streets.

CHAPTER 17

A couple of weeks passed with us living apart and it was going fine for me. Thomas had gotten a room at a hotel that he could pay for weekly and would come over to play with Jacobi every now and then. When he came over he would often try to stay late in order to spend the night, but I worked hard not to give in and had to ask him to leave several times. We still talked to each other every day and made references to us living together again but my mind was made up that I just needed to move back home. One night I went over to Thomas' room to surprise him. He let me in and we talked which led to us making love all night. The next day we spent the whole day in bed and enjoyed each other's company like we used to. That wonderful time came to a halt with a knock on the door by some woman. I was mad, so while he stepped out the door to talk to her, I got dressed quickly. By the time he was headed back in I was heading out past him with no words being exchanged. He followed me trying to give an explanation, but I just shut the car door and sped off. He called for the rest of the day, but I didn't answer the phone. I guess he gave me a few days to calm down and then sent flowers to my job with an apology. I forgave him after he explained that she was someone he and a friend of his who lived in the hotel played cards with. He still didn't convince me enough to let him move back in with me.

In February when I received my tax return it was time to put my plan to leave in motion. It was even easier for me since Angie and her boys were being transferred to Japan and would also be leaving in a few weeks. I told Thomas I was leaving and he confessed his love for me. I loved him too, but not enough to keep going through his drunken rampages. I got a few friends to help me pack and I drove a U-Haul truck to Chicago to my parent's house. My mom had already made arrangements for my furniture to be in storage by the time I got there, so the next day my brother helped me move everything into its temporary spaces. I was a little stressed when I got home because I knew the money I had wouldn't last me forever and I needed to go and look for a job. But I think I was most stressed because I missed Thomas. I didn't think I would, but I had only tried to fool myself into thinking I didn't still love him. We talked everyday for that first week I was in Chicago and then he made a bold move and called my dad. "I would like to come to Chicago to be with Faith and Jacobi. Can I come and live with her at your house? I promise things will be different," he expressed to my dad. My dad and I had already had a long talk about me missing Thomas and thinking maybe things would be different for us in a new environment. My dad told Thomas "I am not for any mess, so don't bring it to my house. I don't get in my daughter's business, but if it's in front of me, I am not afraid to use a gun. Are we clear?" Thomas said "yes" and was on the first thing smoking to Chicago. The first couple of days were a little uncomfortable because my whole family knew that a big part of me moving home was to get away from Thomas and they were happy about it, but then I let him right back into my life and hoped things would be better.

The weekend passed and we had talked a lot about getting jobs so Thomas asked me to take him out to some factories to fill out applications Monday morning. It was draining to hear, "We are not accepting applications at this time," or "just fill it out and we will call you when a position becomes available." We had been out the whole day and were just disappointed after each door closed in our face, but decided to stop at one last place, a printing company. A guy was walking out as Thomas walked in. He asked the guy if he knew if their company was hiring. The guy asked if he had any forklift experience and Thomas told him yes. He then gave him an application and said, "Be here at nine o'clock tomorrow morning." We were so excited and glad that we had made that last stop.

When Thomas went back to the printing company the next day and showed them he could drive a forklift, they hired him on the spot. He would be working in the warehouse moving big boxes of paper cups for different restaurants and companies.

We felt like this is what we needed to be a great couple, but things just were not complete, so we set a date to get married. The move to Chicago was the beginning of a new life for us. The best way to start it was with making vows before God and family, while working to keep them till death do us part. It would happen in September over Labor Day weekend and just before Jacobi was to start kindergarten. We wanted something really small because we're on a tight budget. Thomas and I ended up planning a big cookout for Saturday that both of our families came to. We had barbecued rib tips, chicken, hot dogs, polish sausages, and grilled fish. My mom cooked our side dishes: spaghetti, green beans with ham hocks, potato salad, and toasted garlic bread. Our dessert was a very large sheet cake with teal and white frosting with bell decorations. We decorated the backyard of my childhood home with big helium balloons, different sized bells, and teal and white streamers.

The next day our families packed into cars and drove to Michigan for our wedding ceremony that was being officiated by my Uncle Larry. Jacobi was very handsome in his black suit as our ring bearer. My younger sister, Alysa and Thomas' younger brother, Raymond, made up our wedding party. The ceremony was intimate and short due to a tight budget, but it was more than we expected. Some of my cousins put together wedding favors to give out to the guests, another one sang and did a poem. Our family supported us and was an important part of making this day special for us. That day I felt our lives would shift. I truly loved him and was glad I had given him another chance. We had a small reception, compliments of my uncle and his mother shortly after the ceremony, in the basement of the church. His mom had gone out and purchased us a gorgeous layered wedding cake with bells on top. My aunt and some of her church members prepared a soul food buffet meal that was delicious. Our reception was more like a family reunion, visiting with family members we don't get to see often, and reminiscing of old times. We ended the reception with a toast from the best man and maid of honor, which were both very heartfelt. We all packed up to go our separate ways. Thomas and I left to prepare for our wonderful honeymoon. I was excited!

We were leaving the next day for Florida and then Mexico. My parents would be in charge of Jacobi's first week in a "big boy school." We were nervous but were sure everything would work out just fine.

I was really looking forward to our honeymoon. It was a lot of work putting together the wedding festivities on a tight budget and I could use a vacation to just rest if nothing else. We were in desperate need of some alone time so we invested a chunk of our savings on a beautiful seven-day trip. It was my first time flying so I took a pill to make me rest during the flight, but because I had such a small framed body and not a lot of fat, it made me drowsy the first few days of our honeymoon in Florida. Thankfully, by the time we were to leave for our cruise to Mexico I was well rested and had a great time. The nightlife on the ship was popping; live entertainment, casino, dance clubs, and unlimited drinking. While we were on our cruise Thomas drank from sun up to sun down. I was so focused on keeping him calm and not upsetting him for any reason, that I made sure to remain sober the entire trip. We enjoyed walking the streets and shopping for gifts for our family when we docked in Mexico. On our ship, the captain's dinner was the best. Getting to see Thomas dressed up in a suit and tie was rare so I took a lot of pictures to capture the moments; a black pinstriped suit, white shirt, and a black bow tie. Thomas had on the sharpest black and white-toed gators that rounded out his total look. I wore a long black gown with a white scarf; we looked like the perfect couple. I had a good time, but in the back of my mind I counted each drink Thomas drank, treading lightly to stay on his good side. I was afraid that he would blow up if I said the wrong thing so I said as little as possible. We wrapped up our trip with minimal incidents and headed back home to what I hoped would be new beginnings.

Chapter 18

After we got back from the honeymoon, Thomas went back to work and I started my life as a stay-at-home mother and wife. We returned home more in love and intimate than we had been on our honeymoon. I was missing Thomas each day when he went to work and was eager to show him just how much I missed him once Jacobi was asleep each night. Thomas seemed so attentive to his new bride and I found joy in how much time he was spending with his family. One day in October I woke up feeling horrible. The pain in the top of my stomach was so bad that I could hardly breathe. Thomas stayed at home to try and take care of me, but we had no idea what was wrong. He went to the store and got me an antacid and Tums thinking it was heartburn, but they didn't work. Thomas finally called his mom who was a nurse during her time in the military, to see if she was able to give any suggestions on what was causing me extreme pain and nausea. Thomas went back to the store to get me some soup and tea, hoping maybe it was just a bug that would pass after a few days, but when he came back he also brought a pregnancy test. I thought he was being ridiculous and said I would get up to do it first thing in the morning. When I took the test, as soon as the urine started hitting the stick the color changed to a bright pink. Any type of pink meant I was pregnant. A baby, right now, was not planned at all. Was I ready to be a mom again? So many thoughts ran through my head, but when the shock passed and reality set in there were really no options- we would be having a child within the next nine months. The fear of Thomas' past behavior reoccurring had me a little shaken about adding a new baby to the mix, but ultimately we were excited. I just couldn't help but pray that our life in Chicago would be better than before.

Thomas had made new friends at his job and enjoyed hanging out some evenings and weekends. It was okay as long as he respected that he was now a married man and had a pregnant wife at home. One night he went out and by the next morning had not returned home. My parents and I were emotional wrecks. We thought maybe he was in an accident or had even gotten lost because he was still learning his way around Chicago. My father wanted to call the police, but we waited. My mom and I decided to take a drive around town to see if we saw my car. Chicago is so big and we didn't know the first places to look so we started at his job. We then drove past several clubs and hotels looking for my car or signs of my husband, but still did not find him. By the time I got home I was so embarrassed. My family didn't know that this is something that I go through all the time with him, but I thought things would be different here since this was not his hometown and he only knew a few people. I talked my father out of calling the police and finally about mid-afternoon the next day, he came sauntering in like he had done nothing wrong. My parents both jumped all over him and when he got to me I started. He gave a sob story about getting drunk at a friend's house and not wanting to drive home drunk. After being mad for only a couple of days I forgave him, again. What else could I do? I felt like

I couldn't put him out of the house, where would he go? He only knew my family and a few friends. So as usual, we tried to resume life; working to gain back any normalcy we had started to gain after the wedding.

By now I had started volunteering a couple of days a week at Jacobi's school. I always enjoyed educating children and took advantage of any opportunities I could to do so. Jacobi's teacher was great at her job and took full advantage of having me as her parent volunteer. I worked with small groups of children teaching them to read and exposing them to new math concepts. I helped as much as possible with classroom procedures and even helped her grade assignments. I started out volunteering here and there, but by the end of Jacobi's kindergarten year I was working in his class almost more than the paid teacher's assistant. Ms. Gamble, Jacobi's teacher, took time to teach me all she could about the teaching profession. I absorbed so much knowledge from her and was so happy that a teacher that not only cared about her job, but also loved kids played such an important part in laying the foundation for Jacobi's education. At Jacobi's kindergarten graduation, I wobbled across the stage at nine months pregnant and received flowers and an award for Parent Volunteer of the year. It felt great and I loved those kids like they were my own.

Chapter 19

Thomas, Jacobi, our new addition, Thomas Jr. and I ended up living with my parents far longer than I expected. One of the reasons we stayed so long was because I was afraid to move. I didn't really know what Thomas was capable of. Every time we would start looking at houses I would come up with an excuse like "let's wait until spring" or "it's too cold in the winter months." We also stayed because as Jacobi entered first grade, his school offered me a full-time position as a paid teacher's assistant. I guess someone had seen me work hard and felt I could be an asset to the team. Ms. Gamble and I had become good friends so when I started at the school I became the full-time assistant in her classroom. The skills and knowledge she displayed as I watched her teach over time made me see more and more what my life's goal would be: to be a teacher.

The four years at my parent's house were a far cry from perfect. Thomas periodically did his disappearing acts and still drank all the time. He did stop drinking liquor every day, but Friday through Sunday was non-stop drinking. One time Thomas was gone until the next day and I had had enough. When he came home, I did my normal screaming routine and he just ignored me and typed on the computer. I started to get even more angry because not only was he disrespectful to me as his wife, but now he was also ignoring me. I got up to head to the bathroom and he didn't even look my way. Before I knew it, I grabbed a piece of clothing line from under the stairs and swooped the rope around his neck from the back. I pulled with all that I had within me and even felt that I had the strength of ten men. My anger took over and my actions were barbaric. His chair flipped over and I started to drag him on the floor in my parent's basement, which was now our small two-bedroom apartment. All the anger, frustration, and rage that had built up inside of me were at the tip of my fingers wrapped around the rope. Each time he tugged, trying to loosen the rope, I pulled harder- I WAS MAD! I didn't stop until he was gasping for air and Jacobi had entered the room. My mom came running down the stairs yelling, "Wait! Wait! What is going on?" She stood right next to me. I felt like I had just been in a fight, out of breath and with my shirt falling off my shoulders. I explained to her as Thomas crawled to sit on the couch with one hand holding his neck. He was taking short breaths trying to regain his normal breathing pattern and staring straight at me and me staring right back. I told her, "I tried to kill him and will do it again if he continues to ignore me when I say I am tired of going through the same thing." My mother tried to sit us down to talk, but at this point there was nothing anyone could say to me. I had enough and needed him to know it. I think he got the point because for the next few days he tried to make up and said, "I better watch out for you because you are stronger than I ever would have imagined."

Finally our journey at my parent's house came to an end. We searched and found our own home. We moved on my mom's birthday into a three-bedroom bungalow style home with an enclosed back porch, full basement, and full attic. I loved my house, but once we moved, Thomas made this transition ready to act a fool. He went out more, stayed late at work, and drank like crazy. I knew that with all of this going on, I desperately needed to get my children and myself into somebody's church. I needed help from my family because I couldn't do this alone. I already tried doing it alone for so many years and it did not work. Growing up, my grandmother kept us in church. We went at least three days a week and even did two services on some Sundays. I grew up knowing the importance of having God in my life, reading the bible, and staying connected through prayer. As I got older, I strayed away from the church thinking I had gone enough as a child to ever have to go again, but now I felt that was a mistake. Many times I would call on Jesus when I needed help or to say thank you when I got through a tough time, but I wasn't spending time like I knew I should which is probably why things weren't getting any better.

Chapter 20

I found myself on my knees praying for my marriage and for Jacobi. As he grew older, Thomas started to become firmer with him, well a little too firm. He yelled or spanked him for almost everything and never had a kind word for him no matter how well he did in school. One day Jacobi told me he thought his dad didn't love him anymore- he started to call Thomas "dad" after we got married. I often found myself standing in a room watching Thomas just get wasted with no concern about his family. I thought, "Why can't he love us like he loves to drink? If only our names were Heineken or Hennessey we might have a chance because he loved them without a shadow of a doubt."

I refused to give up on my marriage. I fought for it, not just for me, but also for my kids. They should be given the chance to grow up in a home with two parents that loved them just like I had. I worked to keep them sheltered from the life I had become accustomed to with Thomas, a life with drinking, staying out, yelling, screaming, and then making up. I did know that it would be only a matter of time before Jacobi would be old enough to see through my laughter and smiling at family dinners and see the heartbreak that I lived with each day.

My job as a teacher's assistant kept me living in another world each day as I went to work. Dealing with people who respected me and encouraged me was a breath of fresh air and something I needed to stay sane. I enjoyed my job so much that I decided to make some bold moves towards establishing a future for my family and I. I went back to school. I studied to get my Associates Degree in Early Childhood Education. Going to classes twice a week was a well-needed distraction and to my surprise Thomas supported me. He enjoyed taking care of Thomas Jr. and really had done it anytime he was available since he was born, so he often looked after both boys in the evening while I did homework and studied. I worked hard in school and made the Dean's List each semester I was there. I was one of the oldest people in most of my classes, but those young people had to work hard if they wanted to compete with me. For me, this was more than just getting a certificate; this was something I had started years ago, but didn't complete. I was also the first of my parent's children to be in college and wanted to make my family proud.

My mom and I talked more now that I moved out than we did when I lived with them. She often calls just to give me words of encouragement, which I really appreciate. Now that I'm older and starting to raise kids of my own, I see why my mom had to be tougher on us than we thought she should be. She had to keep our family running smoothly when my father was not taking care of business. She not only had to endure the craziness he sometimes brought to the table, but also juggled the needs and wants of five children, like only a mom can. All of her high expectations were teaching me to become a woman; a woman that would be able to withstand many things and not give up. She often shared things about her life that were a surprise to me, but looking back I can see how they shaped her into the phenomenal woman she is. Her no-nonsense attitude allowed her to deal with my dad all of the years of their marriage and raise children that she could be proud of. If only I would ever gain the strength of my mom- I could conquer the world. Instead, I was left to fight with all that I had to have a dysfunctional marriage and raise two boys in Chicago where the streets preyed on them like rare meat.

My dad dropped by our house anytime he was in our area to bring me something he picked up for me while he shopped for himself. Not much has changed over the years; my dad still spoils us and I wouldn't have it any other way. His relationship with Thomas was okay. He often expressed to him how he felt about his disrespectful behaviors, but said his daughter had to choose for herself who she wanted to spend her life with. They would drink a couple of beers together, but my dad kept it at a minimum and I think he did that for me.

Chapter 21

Work and school were going great and time was passing so quickly. After graduating with my Associate's Degree, I decided to continue on and pursue a Bachelors' Degree in Elementary Education. Thomas felt like the first degree was enough, but after all of the years of ups and downs with him I didn't know what my future would hold and needed to work for my own way to best provide for my children.

By this time in my life, I had totally given up drinking. There was no way I could go on asking Thomas not to drink if I went on doing it myself. It was so easy to stop I didn't miss it at all. We went some months with Thomas doing his regular drinking occurrence, which would end with us going into heated arguments that lasted for hours. These arguments would lead to him saying the most hurtful things that a person could ever say to another person. I felt that he sat and pondered on what he could say to dig deepest into my heart so that I would feel this hurt long after his words stopped. I would stay secluded in my room hoping that the torment would stop, begging for him to leave me alone and just go away.

Thomas started a different shift at work that required him to work overnight which I didn't like very much, but he had to do what it took to help provide for our family. Sometimes I would come home from work or school to find Thomas drinking which means he could have begun when he got off at 7:30 that morning. Since I worked every day, he started drinking whenever he wanted to while he was at home which I was totally against. I was often appalled that he would drink at that time of day. Of course I never said anything because I knew it would result in him saying something demeaning and belittling to me. Diminishing my self-esteem is what seemed to really make him feel like a big man.

One day, I came home at 2:00 in the afternoon after a half day at school and as I pulled down my street I could see Thomas sitting on our front porch. As I parked, I saw one of our blue cups sitting next to his feet and could hear the music blaring from the house. I rolled up the window, sat in the car, and took a few minutes to say a little prayer:

Lord Jesus,

Please protect me from any hurt or harm that could come to me by the hands of my husband. Please keep me safe Lord and keep him away from me. Lord Jesus please stop him from drinking Lord, take the need and wants for alcohol away from him. Lord please guide his mind and prevent him from having evil thoughts that will drive him to saying disturbing things to me that will hurt me for a lifetime. This prayer I ask in your name. Amen.

After this I got out of the car, said hello, walked past him, and went into my room closing the door behind me. I wanted to lie down because I was tired so I went back outside and asked him if I could turn the music down just a little bit. He didn't answer, but got up and turned the music down a little and went back outside. I went back in my room and didn't say anything else to him. I lay in the bed and said "Thank you Lord, thank you Lord." Soon after that he came and stuck his head in the room and said "Can I say something to you without you getting upset?" I knew what that meant. He was about to start saying unnecessary stuff to me because that is how all of our arguments would start. He started by saying that if he wanted to listen to music that it should be his choice and that usually I am not home during this time so that is my problem. But, of course, that did not stop our dialogue. I tried to get him to leave me alone by just saying, "I am sorry, I am sorry." My apologies just made him madder because he then started to get irritated with me. I just sat and listened to him go on and on about me asking him to turn the music down, but not responding started to agitate him. He said that it wasn't his fault that I was tired. That he didn't tell me to go back to school and that I didn't have to do it. Like a dummy, I gave in and spoke just figuring that I could get him to see that I was trying to better myself so that we could have a better life. What was I thinking? He started screaming that I would be the only one to benefit from me graduating and that he could care less if I finished or not. This really hurt me because everything I do is for my family and it hurt for him to say I was only doing it for myself. He kept walking to the front of the house as if he was done talking to me, but that would always be short-lived because he would soon come back and say something harsher than what he previously said. By this time I was begging him to please leave me alone and asking, "Why are you bothering me?" I eventually told him that if he didn't want to be with me it was okay to just leave. He agreed, but said he wouldn't leave until he found a job in another state or found some place new to live in Chicago. I really felt that he was never going to stop talking. He took his wedding rings off, threw them at me, and kept hollering for me to answer him when he wasn't even asking questions. I told him I wanted to die; I felt that was the only way out. Not just out of our argument, but out of our marriage. I ran to the bathroom and locked the door. By this time I was crying uncontrollably and going through the cabinets collecting pills that I could swallow to end all of this madness. I was praying and asking God to forgive me for taking my own life, but I had asked him over and over again to get me away from the madness that was Thomas and things had not worked on my behalf. He started banging on the door and told me if I didn't open it he would kick it in. I believed him because before we moved to Chicago he had kicked down the door in both of our previous apartments, so I opened it and ran to my room. I had the pills in my robe pocket and started to write a goodbye letter to my parents because I needed them to understand that taking my life was the last resort to a situation that I could no longer endure. He came in and snatched the paper from me saying that even if I wrote it they would never get it. All they would get was a dead daughter (which he said while laughing). Each time he would leave I would start writing again. Finally he took all pens from around me and tore my robe off of me so he had all of the pills that I had put in my pockets. I cried like a crazy person and could not stop. He got flustered with me and said, "You want to die? You want to die? Okay, go ahead, I will help you." He started throwing the bottles of medicine and vitamins at me and finally came in and tossed a huge butcher knife in my lap and told me he was now looking forward to me finishing the job. I started saying I wished my kids were there with me because I needed someone with me that really loved me. In between yelling for Thomas to leave me alone I screamed for God to help me. He asked me what my children would do for me if they were there and apparently God couldn't hear me; maybe I should scream a little louder. I finally pushed past him trying to leave the house. He stood in front of the door laughing at me as I tried to go around him and even underneath him crawling in between his legs. Finally he sat down, snapping his fingers to the blaring music and I ran to my car. I picked Jacobi up from school and then went to pick up Thomas Jr. from daycare. I decided we would go to the lakefront for a couple of hours in hopes that Thomas would be sleeping when we got home since he did have to go to work. I was correct, later when we got home, the music was off and he was sound asleep in our room. I shut the door and begged the kids to be quiet so they wouldn't disturb him and he wouldn't move until it was time for him to get up to go to work.

Chapter 22

In order for me to graduate I had to go through student teaching. This would be really hard for me because during this time I would not be able to work. I had saved some money in anticipation for this time, but would still have to depend on Thomas more than ever before. During this final year in school I worked harder in school and on my marriage. Hard work in school had gotten me several scholarships, which really helped our family. My continuous dedication to learning all that I could and displaying a work ethic that made my teachers proud also got me a job offer to a new school that would be waiting on me once I graduated.

Before graduation I had the tests of my life. I had to pass three tests to become a certified teacher and they were extremely difficult. I had never been a good test taker and being older sure didn't help my memory. My other tests came in my household. Did I want to continue the life I had lived for years? Did

I want to have my boys continue to see me cry? Had I given my marriage all that I could with no compromise from Thomas? I was fed up; I just didn't have the energy anymore. I loved Thomas so much, but had to start loving myself more. Thomas still drank as much as he wanted and often rubbed in my face that I would never leave him.

I started to watch a weekly church program on Sundays from home and most Wednesday nights. This pastor stirred up so many things that I remembered from attending church with my grandma that I was shocked that I even allowed myself to get so removed from my foundation. Thomas refused to watch with me, but would often joke and say he hoped the pastor was talking about submitting to my husband.

In only a few months, I would begin a new phase in my life as a teacher. The last semester was tight financially, but my professors helped me get a part-time job on campus. I didn't need any additional stress added to my marriage. Maybe it was time for me to think of other new beginnings. I thought of what life could be like on my own as a single parent raising two boys alone. I didn't believe that Thomas would help me at all since he only visited and talked to his other three children back in Tennessee a few times after we left. I could only hope things would be different, but there was no certainty.

During my finals, Thomas and I got into a terrible argument when I asked for some time to study. He yelled, got in my face, and even tried to physically remove me from the house. I screamed at him, begging him not to put me out. He did anyway and then turned up the music so he couldn't hear me saying I was sorry and that I would just study another time. My boys came to the screen door and stared at me crying on the steps. Thomas didn't let me back in until Thomas Jr. started crying for me. He opened the door and pushed him out with me. Jacobi came and unlocked the door so we could get back in. That was it for me.

Chapter 23

My graduation was only one week away and I wanted so much for this to be the time of my life. It had taken eight years to get my Bachelors' degree and instead of planning a celebration my mind was on getting away from Thomas for good. He said he would not be attending my graduation or anything else for me. As usual, all I did was cry and wait on him to finish screaming that I would never amount to anything. But, things were about to change for me. I was tired of begging him to love me. My mom always said, "You can make a man do a lot of things, but you cannot make him love you." I believed her.

I woke up on graduation day extra early and went straight for the window to see what the weather was like. As I noticed the gray clouds and drizzle falling, I slowly started to feel a heavy weight on my shoulders. Our graduation is being held outside on the school grounds, this is the first time they have done this in years. My whole family, except for my brother, is planning to attend. Not only is it cloudy, it is also 35 degrees and windy. My family is calling because they are concerned about the kids being cold and I am not even sure if I want to attend myself, but I have to see this through to the end. The only driving force I have behind continuing to get dressed is the fact that my boys are so excited for me that I can't let them down.

Thomas woke up this morning getting dressed and saying that he is going to my graduation even if I did give his ticket to my sister Angie who came from out of town just to be with me. I am not sure how the day will end, but right now I have butterflies in my stomach because I know today is the beginning of my new life.

The graduation was wonderful. The bleachers were filled to capacity at the beginning of the ceremony. Periodically, I would look to see my family all bundled up close to each other trying to stay warm. Right before they called my name, my family had retreated inside the building trying to stay shielded from the cold. Other families had done the same; the stands were almost empty. I really appreciated my family being there for me on such an occasion, being the first of my siblings to receive a college degree made my family proud. When I walked across the stage I looked out to wave at my friends who were also graduating and to my surprise my whole family was back in the cold screaming and cheering for me like I was their top celebrity.

I am now a proud Northeastern Illinois graduate with a Bachelors' Degree. My hard work paid off and I graduated with high honors. Thomas was able to get into the graduation because one of my classmates had an extra ticket, but from what I was told he sat in silence. He had no conversation for my family and they had none for him. They were tired of seeing me sad and depressed and if they only knew the things he said to me when he was drinking I would probably be going to visit my dad in jail. After graduation all of us went back to my parent's house where my father put together a fantastic barbecue. We took pictures, danced, and really enjoyed each other. Later on my friends came by to hang out and we just spent hours talking about old times and our futures.

As things were wrapping up, my father felt that it was time for the family to gather around so that they could share a toast with me. I thought it was very nice that they had taken time to make sure that I had sparkling grape cider and that there was enough so that the children were able to join in. My father gave his famous toast that we all looked forward to, "This is to you, this is to me, and I hope that we never disagree. But if we do disagree then forget about you, this is to me." My sisters each shared with me how proud of me they were and that they loved me. I felt the tears welling up in my eyes and a lump forming in my throat, but I held back the tears long enough to allow my mom to take the stage. She looked at me and said, "They say you get two adult lives and when I come back for my second adult life I want to be just like you, I love you." The tears started to flow and I could no longer hold them back. I had people passing me tissue from each part of the room. That meant so much to me coming from my mom. All these years I never knew if I was making her proud. She would say she loved me, but I didn't know how she felt about the decisions I made throughout the years until now. I hugged her so tight that it seemed like life for me at that time stood still. Memories of my past flew in my mind, when I left home, when I moved out of town, when I came back, when I moved into my own house. Am I as proud of my decisions as my family is saying they are? I can't say that I am. I have been unhappy so many years, fighting a battle against someone with a bigger arsenal. I always believed that love would conquer all and still believe that I will be loved the same way I love others.

It was now my turn to speak and I first started with saying thank you to everyone for enduring the terrible weather that day and for going to my graduation. I told everyone how much I loved them and appreciated their support. I hugged and kissed the cheeks of my boys telling them I appreciate them for sacrificing mommy time when I had to study, but that it would get better now that school was over. The only words I had left were for Thomas. As I started to address him, he had a huge smile on his face. "Thomas I love you so much and want to say thank you for being with me while I got through this difficult journey of being a student, mom, and wife. Through all of this we have had good times and bad times, but now our bad outweigh the good and I am tired." As I finished my sentence his smile started to vanish but I continued, "I no longer want to be married to you. I can no longer take you belittling me and making me feel like the scum of the earth. I am tired of this and ready to move on and start a life of real happiness." A hush fell over the room and my dad had come to stand close to me with his hands gently holding mine. I continued, "If you would have only taken the time to love me like that," I pointed as he tightly held a glass of champagne like it was all that he had in the world "we could have worked, but since you chose drinking over me and the children, I hope you are ready to live with your decision. Your bags are packed and in the trunk of the car. I love you, but I am no longer in love with you. I wish you well and there is a taxi cab outside waiting to take you where ever you need to go." He looked in my eyes and stepped towards me where my sisters were now standing and said I should have told him how I felt before he spent his money on roses for me for my graduation. He walked to the door of my parent's house with Thomas Jr. crying and hugging him and told him he would call him later as he hugged him tightly. My sister's boyfriend got my keys and walked him out to get his bags from the car. I stood on the porch with my boys underneath each one of my arms, crying. He looked back at me before getting in the cab and said, "Good luck on your new life." All I could say was, "Thanks," with a lump in my throat the size of an apricot. The words spoken out loud were full of anger and hurt, but underneath I was praying and asking God to please help me on this new journey I was about to embark upon. I still had doubts about the decision I was making, but needed to stand firm behind the choice I had just made. As I planned for this day, I thought about the fact that our house and all of the bills were in my name. How that happened I never thought about before. I had packed the car the night before as he drifted off to sleep after a few beers. His dress clothes had been neatly hanging in the closet for weeks anticipating my graduation and well before he had changed his mind. A few pieces of his things remained at the house, but I can't believe he didn't realize most of his stuff was gone.

Filled with uncertainty and fear I just wanted to be happy.